CHAPTER ONE

"Call the doctor! He's gaining consciousness, he's moving!" A loud vehement outcry of joy suddenly burst on the other side of the bed as we caught a glimpse of his blankets shaking.

"Hurry Jay! Please!" Mom instructed.

I hurried like a whirlwind to Doctor Dube's office, with a banging unwilling heart and a grave countenance in a weighty dilemma of whether or not I needed my cousin to survive. "Doc, he moved! Please come with me........" I screamed without even knocking, and with only my head peeping inside his office while my body lingered outside.

Doctor Dube did not delay but rapidly grabbed his kit and trailed behind me to the male wards where we found mom and aunt kneeling beside the bed holding Sydney's bandaged hands and trying hard to serve hope to his desperate soul. His big hazel eyes were wide open and slowly roaming around the whole ward and they came to a halt as soon as they caught my presence. I knew he was astonished to see me near his sickbed and it did not stupefy me. As much as I was his unexpected visitor, I liked being there with him. However, I was also devastated by his current state of anguish. He was writhing in pain as if some unknown entity was crucifying him. He was bandaged all around the face and his whole body was bandaged too, only his eyes were visible.

"Alright, all of you may now go wait on the bench in the waiting room; I'll check on him and inform you once I'm done. You don't have to worry, he'll be okay", encouraged the doctor as he moved closer to my cousin's bed to examine his condition. I threw a last calm glance at him before closing the door behind me. He followed me with his pale, hopeless and teary eyes and I could not stand the pain I read in them. I was utterly angry with him at some point, but the large part of me tended to completely disagree with me. The only feeling that intensified within me was the endeavor to bury the hatchet with him before he succumbed to his sickness, my guilt would be cleared and it was going to be an easy life again, and wounds and complicated memories would be erased perhaps. Forgiving myself was going to be like taking candy from a baby after pouring my heart out. I close the door, after a session with my brain, and trailed behind mom and aunt as we dragged ourselves unwillingly toward the waiting room and joined others whose hearts were careworn for their loved ones like us. Aunt could not stop sobbing and I knew I had to be strong for her even though perfect guilt was victimizing me, I was still perfect in their eyes hence planting the courage in them through the scriptures was still a walk in the park for me.

"Aunt it's alright. God promised that if we call upon Him in the day of trouble, He will deliver us and we will glorify Him." I rubbed her back comforting her as we sat down on the bench.

"God's watching aunty please calm down. This too shall pass."

"He's my only son Jay, the only fruit of my womb. What is God punishing me for? If he takes him away from me what else will He leave me with? God is supposed to be fair" Her words came out as painful sobs.

"I believe that Sydney will recover soon, it's something I feel within me," I assured and I saw her attempting a smile but could not fake it, instead that smile turned into a loud mourning and everybody gawked at us, some with sorrowful eyes and some with that 'can't you see you're making noise' type of looks. Mom was silent all that time. I kept stealing glances at her, because starring at my mother's eyes was something that scared me a lot, the tranquil soul she was, stoic and taciturn. Her character and her belief in me were thorns in my paw. She had this beauty inside of her, this kindness, and the pride that she had managed to raise at least one of her two daughters in a praiseworthy way; me. She was the reason why I wanted so bad to detest Sydney. I cringed at his thought of ever planning a visit to our place, wreaking havoc, and also awakening sugary feelings in my heart. Mom loved Sydney too; however her love for me outweighed hers for Sydney and everybody knew that I was her favorite person.

"Maybe we should pray aunt."

"Good idea baby," she said tearfully as she quickly knelt on the cold floor and mom did the same. I knew I had to make a more comforting prayer for them because they both believed I was one closest person to God since I held a high and respected position in the church, I had never done anything dense enough to demolish their hopes in me, except that intense hatred I had for Sydney which nobody understood. They were trying every day to make me open up about every day under the carpet and give stupid complicated reasons. I knelt and prayed.

'Father in the name of Jesus we bow before You right now, You know our situation better than us. You are our only hope, our refuge in this time of trouble, comfort our hearts, and help us to keep our faith in You because Lord You promised to never leave us comfortless. In the name of Jesus, I pray, believing that my cousin will get out of his deathbed and claim his place again

3

in the affairs of life because the devil doesn't have power over You. Amen.'

As I opened my eyes, I caught my mother caressing me with her eyes and only heaven knows for how long she had been staring at me, Aunt was smiling too in tears.

"Baby I knew I could count on you, you always lighten up my heart you know. You are a godsend, sent to plant hopes within our failing minds." Aunt said wiping away the tears from her eyes and returning to her seat with a little glow.   "She's a heroine this one Maggie, I always tell you she has solutions to every problem." Mom spoke up, laughing; those were her first words since my arrival. It relieved me so much to have that strong ability and intelligence to cheer their spirits up in troubling times and the title 'Heroine' made me feel blessed, especially coming from my mother. However, it made me feel guilty too, because it gave me so many responsibilities- the responsibilities of a heroine that I scarcely found during self introspection. I knew, however that my mother loved me that much; she would compliment me until she ran out of all perfect words to portray me.

"And I never disagreed with you Laurie," aunt said openly adoring me too with her eyes. I could not stop smiling, gratefully enjoying raining compliments that freshened my soul.

"You know, ever since her father passed away, she's been nothing but a solace to me, my Jack left me with an angel and I'll always love him for that. She heals all my wounds Maggie, she's a blessing unlike Janet, that child gives me too many problems and I don't even know what to do with her anymore." Mom said with a look of anxiety across her face, which was how she responded every time Janet's name was brought up in a conversation.

Aunty laughed and said, "at least you've got Jay; now you believe that God doesn't give us problems without solutions right? Jasmine is the reason why I would love to remarry someday." I held my mouth with both my hands in disbelief, Aunt had given up on love after her boyfriend, and Sydney's father impregnated and abandoned her to be a single mother.

"But I'll definitely get married after I see her in her wedding gown with the most wonderful man ever! I believe that's a few years from now," she said gazing at me and I got stuck in the moment as I remembered how much I always dreamed of a wedding, Initially I had thought would get married to the most desirable and Godly man alive, but I was no longer sure whether that dream was still possible, I had somewhat scratched the beauty of it.

"English says don't count your chickens before they are hatched ma'am, the devil was once an angel remember." A man in a black suit shouted to my aunt from the corner, I turned to look at him, he was carrying a stick and had all sorts of animal skins tied around his neck and hands. He was the physician from our area who was known for being an all-knower and number-one gossipmonger.

"Isn't that jealousy I'm smelling sir?," Aunt said in a bragging and mocking tone. I got all tongue-tied and guilt pierced my soul into pieces, fierce thoughts got hold of my brain and I felt the uncontrollably tingling sensations in my head. I twitched on the chair and cleared my throat endlessly. A guilty conscience needs no accuser, they say.

The man laughed, "Why in the world would I be jealous ma'am? I have kids who disappointed me when I trusted in them, and I no longer see it necessary to praise a child, teenagers will always be teenagers to me and their mistakes will never come to an end"

"Sir, they say teenage is what you make it." I defended myself with a confident voice, seeing mom and aunt were drowning on the man's elements of truth. Mom winked at me and grinned, proud that I also did have the wisdom to defend myself everywhere.

"Alright, alright my daughter, I get your point. If you trust and believe in yourself, you'll make it without a doubt. Just don't let your parents praise you too much while you're filling their eyes with dust so they can't see through you." He exhaled the truth and fueled my sleeping anger, awakening a mean, vicious guilt within me. "I don't love that tone sir, you don't know her well, so don't judge. I just won't let you threaten my daughter in front of me. You're also insulting my upbringing of my kids if you think she's blemished like your daughters, we aren't the same remember?" boiled mom, the skin on her forehead flipping in a frown.

"Calm the hell down madam! I didn't mean to offend anyone, I was just stating my reasons why these teenagers can't be trusted. It was just a lesson to your youngster, nothing more. However don't say I didn't warn you when expectations start hurting you. I wish to be there on that particular day." His rude lips curled in a smile and his eyes mocked.

"Yeah, that's true, that's what you do with people's lives, and you take nonsense from your useless stupid bones and think you're God to predict our destinies, no man we don't believe in all your nonsense, your witchcraft won't work with us. You want to practice it on our daughter as you did with all your kids, this God we serve won't allow you to, just go to hell!," aunt started raging and I noticed beads of sweat running down her chubby cheeks. She wiped them off with a towel and breathed heavily, she was boiling inside. She was a no-nonsense type of a woman and was known to hit both men and women when furious and I saw it in her face that she was finding it hard to calm down.

"Point of correction woman! I'm a physician and not a witch, but I also have wisdom about life and God. I heal people not kill them or poison them, why in the world would I spoil my kids? That's an insult too."

"Get the hell away from us you stinking pig," aunt grabbed him by one hand and pushed him back while pinning him to the wall. "If you don't leave from here I'll kill you with my bare hands".

"Help!," the man mewed like a cat as he fell down, head first to the floor.

"Next time learn to live in your world, stay in your lane and mind your own business," mom rescued him by seizing aunt's hand and sitting her down on the bench.

"Don't mind these people Maggie, they've been hating on us for years but Jasmine is still the same. What people do is talk, nothing else," mom said in a consoling tone.

"I hate him, he pissed me off. I'm hurt and he's adding coals, I'll kill him," aunt exhaled loudly. We glued our eyes to the man as he came and sat down on his chair, embarrassed. He calmly gathered his bag and fronted the opposite direction from us. He veered around for a second and stared at me then looked away; I just twisted my mouth and rolled my eyes while feeling the needle sinking deeper into my soul. What if that man was smelling some fish in my water? I wondered.

"Time for the second patient's visit, you may all go inside," the doctor interrupted the silence among us. We all stood up and headed to different wards where our loved ones were admitted, I saw the man in a black suit disappearing to a female ward and I followed him with my eyes his words still stuck on my mind, I ignored them and pushed them into the corner.

'Adults will always are adults,' I thought. We uttered a prayer before opening the door, fearing to be greeted by an empty mattress and then slowly dragged ourselves in, as afraid as grasshoppers. Sydney was sleeping alone in the side-room because his condition was worse than the patients who were grouped in one ward. He pivoted his head a little to look at us and tried to smile. No longer covered with blankets, his steel muscles showed up a little and he was clad in a blue hospital gown. We were all happy to see him still alive. I moved closer toward him.

"You're going to be okay cuz, I believe so. I see a difference in your state from that of earlier." I said, holding his pale hand and offering him a dull smile. He stared at me with a confused face. I would not stop scanning his body from head to toe and my attempts to ignore him proved to be in vain. How could I ignore his full and pinkish lips that looked so becoming just above the bandage that wrapped his chin up to the head. His light complexion illuminated the hospital gown that he wore, and the room as a whole. His body had become even stronger; muscles and veins had multiplied and bundled up his body mercilessly. All hairy and muscular, he looked exactly like those adorned actors I used top see on television and magazines. With that kind of a body, I wondered how he even failed to hold a teaspoon, diseases are just so powerful, I thought to myself. Nonetheless, I could not help but smile as memories of that evil night rained down on my head.

"What are you even thinking about Jay, you won't stop smiling?," Aunt laughed and brought me back to life. I leaped off my chair and let go of his hand faster as I came back to my senses. "And then? You jump as if you have been caught sinning?," she continued

"No aunt, I'm looking at him thinking... that... he'll soon be alright." I faked a giggle, I had just escaped from a disaster of betraying myself.

"You like him now?," she rubbed my back.
"He's my cousin."

"He's your cousin but you hate him. We all know that."

"I don't," I kept my replies short, I had just smiled at Sydney and was wondering why all of a sudden my anger and hatred for him was slowly dying away.

"Maybe your hatred is the reason why my son could not even travel safely. You sounded harsh on the phone, you never wanted him to visit!," aunt said pushing me away, harshly and her words cut deep within me. How could she blame me? I was not responsible for my cousin's accident.

"Come on Auntie! Don't say that," I cried out.

"What do you want me to say huh? Expect me to clap my hands and continue loving you and praising while you hate my son with passion Jay? We stood by you against that man and ignored this fact that you're such a hater; you won't even talk with your own cousin! Who does that? An honorable youth leader? An ordained one of God?." Aunt was a nice person, but could be strict and harsh when provoked. I started shaking at the solemnity of the topic; I was scared of aunt, especially after the way she had behaved with that man. I stared at mom seeking defense and refuge but she threw me under the bus unexpectedly.

"I'm for aunt's point Jay. We don't expect a leader who calls herself God's child to entertain hatred, for her own cousin for God sake, that's weird and insecure. I've warned you several times about this matter."

"And we are not going to warn you further, either shape up or ship out of that higher chair, we'll tell the church elders about this matter!" Aunt reddened with anger and I could not believe mom was also abandoning me like that, I had to choose. "No, why would you do that? It's nothing I can't handle." I tried sounding so calm deep down I was wasting away.

"If it's something you can handle, you should have dealt with it back then, your father's spirit will never rest in peace, and it will come upon you I swear. He tried with all he had to unite both of you when he was alive, my son was willing but you pulled to another direction Jay, you want to separate this family and note that we won't allow you to do that. Over my dead body!" The words about my dad's spirit scared me the most, he too had questioned me about the matter and I had dug here and there, giving numb and dumb reasons, he had passed away peacefully later but the fact that he had died without me confessing the truth to him eroded me inside.

"That's true, you need some time I guess, we'll let the elders hand over the work to someone else while you deal with your hate issues. This is unlike a Christian, a person who has completely offered herself to God and promised to utter no vile word or action against anybody, you're breaking the rules and you'll embarrass us."

Mom has never scorned me before and I understood stoically that my hatred for Sydney had started to tire everybody in my family, including Janet herself. They had all believed in me but it had been difficult for them for those two full years of my insecurity as they would point it. My mother was the last person I needed to disappoint, I therefore convinced my heart to try and get close to Sydney for her sake, which was the only way my family could love me again without any problems. If I had continued hating on him, they would dig deep to the core until they got the yolk of the matter, I would commit suicide, loving him would be better and easier than confessing my secret to them. "But mom and aunt, I'm here today, doesn't that mean I'm willing to try?" I humbled myself with silent agitation.

"All this is pretending Jay, we can see through you. We've been in this world long before you existed, you can't fool us." I could see beads of sweat forming on aunt's face again because of anger.

"I'm sorry for all this then. I really am, I'll try bonding with Sydney." I said with a voice of surrender, accepting I was going to be locked up in that hell of guilt alone since I could not confess my mistakes to them. It scared me much that they were heated by hatred, how were they going to react after knowing the real reason behind it?

"You better be sorry my dear because as far as we are concerned, there is no reason behind your hatred. You used to like him back then but after being ordained your behaviour changed, we won't accept that. We don't even know how he feels about your presence here; maybe it kills him, what if he won't heal. He'll die because of you," aunt would not stop roaring and heating up the matter.

"I've already apologized aunt. I was just being insecure; I didn't see it was troubling everybody. I will apologize to God too. I love Sydney more than anything, he knows that, it was just a minor misunderstanding that made us fight and now I understand that we shouldn't have fought to begin with." I said tearfully with a deep pain of being caught in a serious dilemma.

"Good then, it better stay like that, no more sulking! We so damn tired of all that." Aunt, a chubby and light woman was severe in discipline, Sarah when laughing but Jezebel when restricting, worst part she was in sorrow, all which rained on me.

"I've raised a woman like this; holds no grudges and loves without conditions," mom said with a determined smile. I gave back a dull smile, wishing she knew what exactly had transpired between me and my horrible cousin but relieved that she had accepted without questioning because she trusted me that much.

"Now let's put all this behind us, tell us how is it going at church? I heard them all praising your leadership." Aunt wore a happy face once again; the seriousness in her face had faded. She knew very well I was scared of her and I loved instructions, she knew I would be a sheep after being instructed and she loved me for that.

"It's all well aunt, I've organized youth camp meetings, bible study groups, and even nature walks. The pastor is amazed and relieved." I smiled remembering to bring all the efforts I was putting into my church and also glad to have them changing the topic so suddenly.

"This is the reason why we want you to bond with your cousin, everything will go well and God will protect you even more," mom held my hand; it was just beautiful to have a mother like her.

"I know mom and I promise I'll forgive him and move on." I faked a smile as mom hugged me and aunt smiled along with me.

I sat back in bed, took out my bible from my purse and started reading the verses, I needed something to distract myself from the raging storm in my mind and the bible was the best thing because it relieved my mother to see me with it as she thought I would be busy with church chores. We chatted until Sydney woke up, I would quote a verse and we would argue upon it and I made sure it was verse that planted hope in Sydney's mind.

"It's getting late Maggie we need to go," Mom stood up and grabbed her bag after we've stayed for long and it was darkening in the room and a cold breeze was starting to sweep through the sideward we were in.

"You and Jay can go Laurie; I will stay behind with my son, he can't be alone in this condition. He needs me throughout the night." Aunty said with a low voice, sitting at the back of the bed with her head resting on her left hand, the posture of sorrow. I had to use that opportunity to prove to mom and aunt that I was connecting with Sydney.

"No Aunt, you've been here for long and you haven't eaten or bathed. Go home with mom I will stay behind with him, you'll exchange me tomorrow morning." She turned and gazed at me with disbelief, eyes and mouth wide open.

"What? For real?"

"Yes aunt. You need to be away from this view for some time, breathe and get some fresh air in that way you'll get energy to carry all this with perseverance." Aunt could not help but smile,

I won a trophy in her eyes again. I knew I had gotten the chance I needed, to make them love me and never lose their faith and belief in me, because it would be worse if they did lose all that.

"Jasmine is right Maggie, you need some fresh air." Mom supported my point with her lips curving in a warm smile too.

"This is the Jay I know and love! Welcome back Jasmine." I laughed as aunt progressed and hugged me tight. "Thank you so much my love."

"I want nothing other than peace aunty." I insisted, wishing I could indeed be peaceful in my mind.

"I knew you liked him, the devil was just using you and please don't allow him to, we trust you."

"We'll be fine aunt".

"Sydney baby, we're leaving you with your cousin now, we'll be back early in the morning since you're awoke now. I love you my son, be strong for your mother. Please be nice with her too since she wants to work things out with you." Aunt kissed Sydney's cheek as he nodded his head and smiled.

"I hope you mend ties baby, we have to go." Mom warmed me with a hug too as they turned to leave and I waved.

I closed the door and turned my eyes to look at Sydney, his eyes were glued to the ceiling and I felt like he was ignoring me. I was clueless as where to start with him but one thing for sure I had to make sure I did not worsen his condition. I went and sat opposite to him but kept on throwing fake smiles at him every time he start me. He was still unable to speak so all I had to do was pray all night to give him hope, I was still angry inside but I had to vomit it all out since I had volunteered to be his keeper to please my family.

"I know you're surprised to see me here, I also don't want to be here but as you heard, mom and aunt want us to unite. I'm still angry with you and I don't know if I'll ever forgive you but I'll pretend," with tears flooding down my cheeks I knelt beside him and prayed.

"Father in the name of Jesus I pray. I'm tired of fighting with emotions that never go away, I can't do this alone and if You hide Your face from me, I won't make it. Please show me the way, because I love my cousin. Amen."

He rolled his head slowly and glued his eyes at me completely annoyed by my insanity. I raised mine also and our eyes met and brought back memories of that stained night, the night I had tried living to forget and pretending it never happened. I ignored his eyes after a few minutes and went and sat on a chair and grabbed a blanket that aunt had left in the room.

CHAPTER TWO

I resided with my mother and younger sister Janet at a small township in a four-roomed house. Though it was never so huge, our house was spacious enough to locate the three of us. There was our mother's bedroom, the lounge, our bedroom, a small sized kitchen and the bathroom. Our kitchen was a small-sized one, with a four-plate stove, refrigerator, and two huge cupboards for plates, cups, and other kitchen utensils. The lounge had a table, a television stand, a set of couches and a huge television. In my mother's bedroom was her bed, her dressing table and a fitted wardrobe. My and Jenny's bedroom was also not huge, we shared one bed and a wardrobe. Due to a shortage of rooms, we would sleep on the floor each time we had visitors, especially male visitors. Hygiene was well comprehended in my home since we were Christians and the church we attended enforced laws on hygiene, health and wellbeing of humans, the Seventh Day Adventist church. My mother, Laurie Esther, the wife to the late Jackson Moyo who passed away when I was still schooling, was a nurse in a township clinic and was never earning much but enough for the basics. Dad had worked in South Africa for white people before his death; he was the breadwinner and providing enough for us therefore his death caused a downfall of our home economy but mom was there still striving to give us a better life. Dad had his sister Margret, whom we called Aunt Maggie who lived in Cape Town with his only son, Sydney Dawns. Aunt Maggie was a chubby, rich businesswoman with businesses all over Cape Town or so we heard. His son was a spoilt brat, grew up in royalty with everything he wanted and was studying Law in the University of Cape Town. Aunt and his son were not Christians even though she embraced Christianity a lot because of me, or so she said. She had been heartbroken by her husband, Sydney's father who denied impregnating her and left her while Sydney was still a fetus. Both of them visited us frequently, especially on Christmas holidays and they continued doing so even after dad was no more. We were two close families despite the sadness that we both had lost male figures in our journeys. We were the well-known and well respected family in the area, my mom was a church deaconess and my dad had been the church elder before his exit to his resting place. I was a youth leader, a church chorister and a prayer band leader and was also ordained after a strange choice to dedicate myself to God's work as a result of my love for God loved and because the church loved my peculiar behavior, they saw it fit to dedicate me to God. Janet was not so much into Christianity; she only went there as it was a must for us to, but stopped attending permanently after dad's death. She started drinking alcohol, smoking weed and clubbing hard. She and dad were never on good books even before, he used to beat her up but his attempts to halt her bad habits did not work.

****

I remember life was precious to me on my teenage days; I was quite devoted to Christianity that I preferred my body natural, no artificial beauty. I was my father's beloved and a crown on my mother's head. My parents were so proud of me and my works; I was the child of God and walked so well with Him through prayer and attending church services and Bible study groups every day of my life. I was every peer's enemy and every parent's dream because I was a princess to every church member too. Everybody close to me was waiting forward for my brighter future which I too had waited forward to. While my friends were busy with boys, I was studying harder and used to achieve in all my exams. Women and men in the community envied my parents for having me hence they encouraged my good deeds and cultivated them in every way. I was pictured as a role model to every determined teenager and such praises boosted my pride and my confidence; I became famous for my good deeds and my exemplary behavior. At school, I was the cream and I was appointed to be the Head girl from form two to the upper form. I enforced laws at school which amazed the Headmistress herself, which deepened her trust and love for me. I had no boyfriend nor was interested in any boy.

"I wish every pupil in this school would follow in Jasmine's shoes." The headmistress once addressed the school assembly after we had finished writing our ordinary-level exams and two days before my ordination. My heart melted in relief. "She is one of our best students and we're so proud to announce that this Friday there is a service at church to surrender her to God, you're all invited there to see the rewards of being faithful and trustworthy..." She drew a breath before going on.

"...Instead of roaming around with boys and destroying her future, she chose good characteristics. Good performance, punctuality, smartness, and self-control. I must assure you all that if you learn one or two things from her, you will never go wrong!"

My mates were raged, and the whole school threw back murmurs and mumblings towards the head. 'Jealous pupils' I thought as I moved towards my class after assembly with my face glowing, illustrating the happiness inside my heart.

I was so overjoyed to be allowed to be a leader of all youths in my church. It was a heartwarming experience, an opportunity of a lifetime. Endless smiles kept on radiating across my face as I sat with my parents in my last worldly night.

"Jay my daughter, you know you're the marrow inside our bones and we're glad that it's not only us who sees your holy character but everybody. You're one of the reasons why we progress as proud parents out there, I pray you never disappoint us with this" Dad said, hugging me tight from behind and kissing my cheek.

"I promise to always be considerate of my everyday actions dad. This is a lifetime opportunity, God's grace is upon me." I said tearfully.

"A promise is a credit baby girl; you know how relevant that service is to our church, and it's the night where you'll have to connect with God, seeking His guidance, thanking Him for His blessings, the night of purity and fasting, the night where you deny all worldly lusts and give yourself wholly to God. It's never a walk in the park being a leader; it comes with so many responsibilities. You've got to be always exemplary," he lectured while holding my hands.

"Yes dad, I'm aware of that. Nothing will hinder me to offer myself to God, not even the devil himself. I've made this decision and I'll go for it," I assured him.

"That's alright my dear but you should know that the devil is strong and luring, you can only defeat him by Jesus' name and nothing else," dad said, patting my back.

"That's it dad, I believe God lives within me," my lips curved in a smile and I stood up.

"Will aunt and cousin also be there too?" I asked whining in my dad's arms, it would be a great pleasure having them around for my inauguration and anointing as the Youth Leader.

"Yes my dear, they're coming tomorrow. They can't miss such a great night!" Dad said.

I happily moved towards our bedroom to change. I found my little sister Jenny sitting on the bed applying cosmetics to her face.

"Sis Jay, how are you? I'm starting to feel like Mary the mother of Jesus was totally like you," Jenny said as I entered.

"Well, not so different even though not alike," I giggled enjoying the compliment, and hugged my little sister.

"Yeah right? virgin, pure and holy, seems like you never lack any perfect character. Will you be able to maintain it till the end sis?" Jenny asked as we unlocked from the hug.

"What do you mean? Isn't it easier being good than being bad?" I sat on the bed and removed my socks and school shoes.

"Might be sis, but sometimes I feel like being known as bad is better than being labeled angelic, because if you stumble and fall, people will know that's you and your imperfections, but what happens when an angel gets tainted? With millions of people who believed in her, won't it break hearts?" I observed my little sister as she spoke with such weight.

"Are you somewhat jealous baby girl? Do you think I have skeletons in my closet?" I asked with my eyes widening because I knew I had none whatsoever.

"No! Sis Jay, please don't get me wrong. Why would I be jealous of you? You're my sister and my role model for heaven's sake. I just fear for the day you'll do something wrong. I just feel like it's going to harm you."

"Oh! Jenny, don't worry about me sweetheart, I've made a vow with my parents, that I'll never ever disappoint them and tomorrow I'm going to make a vow, in front of the whole congregation I can't believe this is happening," I closed my eyes as I imagined myself in front of the church telling God 'I'm yours for eternity and will never disappoint You.'

"That should stay that way, because there's nothing more painful than betrayal, you've made them believe in you hence should maintain that path I can't tell about how it's like betraying God; remember Judas had to hang himself as he could not bear the pain of regret. I don't have anything to worry about because mom and dad know I'm not a good child and they've gotten used to that," Jenny said as she continued applying make-up and I chuckled.

"Wow, since when did you become a preacher? I thought you were a club animal and knew nothing about God!"

"My sister, the one and only Jasmine is always telling me about the story of Judas and the bible as a whole." She chuckled too kind of embarrassed that.

"I understand your point dear, but I think when the bible speaks of 'honoring our parents,' it really has something to do with us minding how they feel about everything we do. You cannot expect mom to fall in love with you bringing boys into this house every day against her rules. Besides, you're still young. You're too young to start dating. You should've taken after me, eighteen and chaste!" I said with my hands supporting every sentence.

"I'm trying love, I know mom and dad can see that, but I love you Jay and I know you know that and I believe in you," her lips curved in a smile.

"Thank you my love! I love you too."

"Now promise me that you'll stay like this until you find me a perfect brother-in-law. I too can't wait for your big day, it inspires me a lot and I'll try not to apply any makeup tomorrow," she cracked up.

Janet appreciated me a lot, even though my parents had appeared to be in my favor a lot and the whole area was criticizing her for not learning from me as we stayed under the same roof, she was never moved and was never jealous. Besides being rude she was a heroine and deep inside her laid an innocent cool soul. I would go mad at her every time she went wild but deep inside she was a cool soul.

"I promise to never let you down young sister; you've got to be my best girl in my wedding someday..." we laughed and hugged. I had promised myself to make sure that my feet were in the right direction, for them, dad and everybody who had their eyes on me.

"Now let's stop this movie. I'm going to a party tonight at Sarah's. I need a drink or, two to freshen up my mind from this school nonsense."

"No partying tonight Jenny. You were just preaching to me. We've got to do a spring cleaning!"

"Oh! Damn it! Sis, I just remembered that Aunt and Sydney are coming over."

"Yeah, you know our hygienic aunt and her handsome son." I laughed as I picked a mop and began mopping the floor.

"Girls will be roaming around Sydney tomorrow; could be a sight for sore eyes. I have to be there at your big night," said Jenny as she danced.

"Tomorrow's night is sacred, for worshipping and presenting your requests to God. You should never dare commit some stupid crimes on this day especially that your parents will be worshipping, you might be cursed. No matter how strong and luring the temptation might be, make sure you become irresistible." I warned Jenny seriously.

"But you're right sis, I think I really should make a contact with God, my sins are just too much. I also know that no matter how much of a sinner I am, I have to respect this service. One day cannot rot an elephant, right?"

"Now that's my pretty girl!" I kissed her cheek and her lips curved in a heart warming smile as we proceeded with our cleaning.

Aunt and Sydney's arrival on Friday morning was an ultimate joy for the whole family. We had last been with them the previous Christmas holidays and there was a huge difference in everybody. Sydney had grown so much, with muscles all over his body, a bass in his voice and he was even taller than before. He had finished his matric and was in his first year studying law in the University of Cape Town. Jenny had grown too though she was still cute and diminutive and I, being on the fourth form and on my puberty stage, had several changes too. It was a great delight for the family to meet after such a long time.

"So girls, you need to be ready, it's a very big day for all of us as you know Jasmine will be inaugurated as the church's youth leader. We are also offering her to God," dad said later that afternoon as we all sat for lunch.

"I will be cursed if I miss this special night. I can't wait to hear my angel's beautiful voice." Aunt laughed with a mouthful of pap.

"Trust me; it's going to be the best day ever! I'm the happiest woman alive," mom joined along.

"Is that even possible?" Sydney asked and everybody laughed.

"Everything is possible cousin!" I responded.

"Yeah right, I've never been to church but the way you guys are praising this thing, it sounds much like a hallowed one and I guess I'll have to experience how it feels like." Sydney, he was never a Godly person, he was into the world, fashion, hip-hop and girls were his number one icons.

"You really should go nephew, you might feel the presence of God there, its wonderful trust me," dad said to him.

"I will go uncle, definitely."

"I promise to make you all proud of me," I said.

After, washing the dishes, I bathed and went to help Mrs. Moyo our church deaconess with the preparations for the big day.

"I knew you would be the first one to come princess, but you shouldn't have come. It's your day, you had to be busy with prayers," she said as she hugged me.

"I knew you needed help ma'am it's a big night for me and everybody, the church should be spotlessly clean," I said as I started helping her out with the cleaning and decorating of the church.

Deacons and deaconesses started coming one by one and when night approached, the church members were gathered like sand at church and they all greeted me with warm and lovely greetings, wishing me well on my new path with the Almighty. I shed tears when our pastor came and greeted me too. "Are you ready my dear?" he asked as we shook hands. "Hundred percent pastor, I've never been so delighted before," I said tearfully.

"Good then dear. See you on the platform. We'll start by half past eight, for now it has to be singing," he smiled and left. A pretty feeling that lingered through me made me feel like I was on top of the world. My friends and classmates were all present including Cheryl and Mercy, my closest friends and classmates. The congregation started singing with melodious voices. Many members of different churches were present also to catch a glimpse of my special ordination. Mom, dad, and aunt also approached and found me doing meet and greet with church members.

"Baby, how is it going? Are you okay?," mom asked.

"I'm fine mom. I just need to go back home to grab a jacket, it's freezing cold."

"No baby, it's late already. I don't think that's a good idea." She blocked my way.

"No mom, the pastor said the service will start by half past eight and it's six o'clock right now. I will be back in just a few minutes," I assured her.

"Okay dear, please hurry and don't delay us," she said and let go of my hand and I ran past the crowd towards the gate. I ran out of the church yard like a whirlwind and came in an aggressive collision with someone, it was so hard that my nose bled.

"Hey, I'm sorry. I didn't see you coming, I'm really sorry," I recognized his face; it was our pastor's son. I did not know his name, he usually came to church during the holidays, a proof that maybe he was schooling somewhere of course. He was older than me, judging by his face, height and maturity.

"It's okay, I'm sorry too. Anyway, I have to keep moving," I took one step forward and he blocked my way.

"Wait! I'll feel bad if you leave like this, you're bleeding and you need somewhere to wash your nose, let's go back to church, there's a water tap there. I'll help you wash." He begged.

"Don't worry, I'm on my way home and it's not so far, I'll wash my face there, thank you though."

"Aren't you the one to be ordained tonight? Why would you go back home now?" he persisted.

"Just to collect my bible and jacket, I came here at noon to clean up, so I left everything at home and it's a bit cold out here."

"Don't worry, I have a bible with me and I can give you my jacket. Let's go back please," he grabbed my hand and stared at my face, I was about to agree with him and turn back when Janet and Sydney approached.

"If she says no why won't you respect that?" Sydney growled. "You get lost from here before I kick your behind man."

"It's okay *cuz*, , it's no big deal c'mon." I knew Sydney was treacherous and could hit the poor guy.

"What do you say? Are we going back?" The guy asked ignoring Sydney's anger.

His begging me kind of made me feel anxious, what if he was a temptation placed in my way by the devil? I thought.

"Well, I want to go back with you but I don't think I'll be okay in your jackets. Thank you though. I'll be fine." A whole part of me wanted to return back but I feared people would think I was having an affair with the pastor's son, hence I chose the contrary.

"Okay be safe then," he said as he left.

"She was going to be safe even without your saying so," Sydney mocked rudely and I slammed his mouth a little. "I'll escort you home Jay, this moron might follow you with evil intentions, I'll have to protect you," he said and the guy just scanned him and left.

"Don't worry about me cuz; I'll be back in a few minutes." I progressed and he pulled my hand to stop me.

"This is not up for discussion, Jenny, are you going back with us?"

"No I can't, you guys go back let me meet my friends." Jenny said and ran towards the church as I and my cousin marched back home. "And you really need to bath Jay, we don't want to be embarrassed, you stink," he said as we entered our yard and unlocked the door. "You're just silly, people should employ their senses of smell somewhere for tonight, and I'll still get dirty anyway because prayers might get deep to a point of rolling and tossing." I entered our bedroom and searched for my jacket in the wardrobe while he sat on bed and cuddled with a pillow.

"A pretty and famous girl like you has to be smart and clean. The whole church expects that in you, even the pastor himself will stand away from you if you keep stinking this badly," he persisted until I went and took a quick shower, stepped out and got dressed in my long baggy white dress because I had to respect the service.

"Now your wishes are fulfilled sir," drifting my eyes to show him I was fresh and ready, I noticed he was all dressed up to kill. Dark grey skin-tight and long sleeved t-shirt, showcasing his muscles in all their right places, skinny faded jeans and white sneakers, the dress code you see on American musicians and actors.

"*Cuz*, you don't need to dress up like we're going to some party. You have to respect the Lord's house. You were supposed to being a suit at least."

"I won't be preaching Jay, I'm going just to fulfil uncle's wish, I'm not a church person, you know that," he laughed.

"Oh I see, so my ordination means nothing to you?." I twisted my mouth to the sides and rolled my eyes; he threw the pillow into the bed, stood up and stepped two feet forward and held both of my hands.

"I was just kidding Jay; you know I'd kill a lion with my bare hands just to save you," his pinkish lips curved in a smile as he winked and I blushed a little.

"I need proof of that," I shook myself from his hands.

"Just wish and I'll command," he said, biting his lower lip romantically.

"You'll start attending church service every day with me. You'll be Godly too."

"Oh my God! I saw that coming. I'll do that, from today onwards, I'm a Christian, as long as you're the leader." He moved forward, tied his arms around my waist and kissed my cheeks as I smiled my heart swimming in delight with the news that my bad cousin was repenting.

"Good boy!" I freed myself from him once again when I realized I was getting too comfortable and went in search of my bible in mom and dad's bedroom.

"So you said I should change my clothes right? To respect your holy ordination," he shouted from our bedroom.

"It's not like you have any clothes that you can wear to church cuz, keep those on, no one will notice you," I shouted back.

He slowly marched into my parent's bedroom where I was and leaned on the door.

"Unless you want girls throwing themselves at you the whole night Jenny said. Those muscles, beards and those pink lips will tempt many girls," I said and he smirked, taking it as a compliment.

"Just like they're tempting you now?"

"Keep on dreaming my cousin. Muscles don't define a man. I need a Godly man."

"Let's hope you'll find one but I bet you'll fail just like you're failing to find something you're searching for while I'm looking at it from a distance," he said, moving towards where I was standing and pulled the Bible from the shelf and offered it to me and shook his head, I laughed.

"Oh, you've got sharp eyes, thank you," I said as I turned around and noticed after bumping into his iron-made muscles with my soft hands that he was standing just an inch behind me, shirtless.

"Not sharper than your nipples though, they all out, pointed and…"

"You've gotta stop kidding me right now. That's not cool, don't make comments like that," I could not help the embarrassment and faced the opposite direction and closed my eyes.

"Sorry I can't help but notice them, I mean who wouldn't," he giggled

playfully like a puppy. Opening and lifting my eyes, I caught his big hazel globes caressing me, his chest bare, the rows in his chest shining bright like he had just got a full-body massage. Again I looked away shyly, I was starting to feel uneasy.

"Since my muscles are your temptation they'll have to victimize you," he licked his upper lip and exhaled a bit loudly with a smile streaming across his youthful face. My spirit and flesh, I felt them clearing out of me.

"Cuz let me grab my jacket I don't want to be late, mom warned me not to delay them," I said as I endeavored with my left little powers to ignore the view launched just an inch before my eyes.

"Why are you trying so hard to look away from me?" he shifted me to his direction, pulled me closer until there was no space left between us.

"Sydney, stop these games I don't want to be late man, stop it!" I tried freeing myself but his grip tightened on my waist and he just stared down at me. I could hear his breaths getting louder and could feel him getting hotter, as much as I was naïve about such situations, I knew something was not right, in my body too.

"We'll leave in a few minutes Jay come one was still have a lot of time. Don't you enjoy being alone with me as much as I enjoy being alone with you?" he asked with a low tone.

"We'll be alone Sydney, we're always alone." I gave up on my attempts to free myself and simply chuckled.

"You're too much Sydney, why are you like this?" I rolled my eyes.

"Jay," he muttered lowly.

"Yeah?," I raised my eyes and stared up at him and found his eyes full of affection and fondness.

"I know you love my body and I know you wish for a man with muscles like mine."

"What are you on about?" I asked laughing at his serious face.

"Well, Jenny told me you think I have a nice body," he smiled.

"Well, she was just bluffing, boosting your ego I guess." I proceeded with my laughing without caring about the solemnity of the matter.

"Enjoying the hug?" his voice was disturbing my vow of trying to ignore whatever was luring me into temptations.

"Can you let me go now?..." I said with a low tone, I did not realize that my voice was also starting to fail me. He tightened his arms around my waist, I lost my breath feeling his lips on my neck. "Let's go now Sydney, everybody must be...."

"Shhh..." his bass and honey-filled voice commanded lust and respect as his index finger rested on my already wet lips after we unplugged from that long and tight hug.

"Sydney...."

"I know very well that you need this just the way I do Jay, your body language is speaking so loud and I want to listen and submit to it. You love me and you want a sip of me just as much as I want a sip of you. Don't deny yourself this feeling baby." He kept on brushing my lips softly with his fingers and the warmth was aggravating inside my veins and my voice box was condemned. Failing to resist the temptation, I surrendered all of me to him, I threw my bible on my mom's bed and gripped his muscle tightly as he observed me affectionately and tenderly. I laid my head onto his muscular bundle and his lips curved in a honeydew smile, I had never witnessed such a becoming man, he was handsome I could eat him with both my hands and never get satisfied. I had never experienced that kind of warmth in my body, it felt so ethical, felt so legal. He closed the small space between us by fastening his hand around my waist and I moved and my body submitted to his commands. "Still want to roll baby?" He affectionately mocked while his right-hand tenderly fondled my cheek, at that moment I wanted to be engulfed.

"I don't know," I said softly.

"That sounds like a no. I don't want us to roll, I want us to live here alone, just me and you till time stands still."

He planted a gentle kiss on my cheek, I unlocked my hand from behind him and pinned them onto his head with my lips slowly parting as his descended onto them, locking us to that warm heaven for minutes, melting my limbs and electrifying my whole innocent body, staining my untainted soul. He was taking on them slowly, sucking on them like he was sucking some delicate object. While I still enjoyed swimming on that ocean, he plucked the sweet out of me and I opened my eyes blaming, begging that he proceeded with the fairy tale bliss.

"Jay, I love you." He said with a deliciously faint voice and I could not help but watch with affection such a god of a man announcing them three weighty words with a such strong attachment. "I've always loved you, every time I visit all think about is you. I always want you," he emptied, with loud heavy exhales, I wanted him not the talking, I had nothing to say.

"I love you even more Sydney." My eyes blurring even more, I emptied my whole soul into his and wished with all my within that Sydney remained glued to my spirit the way he was with my body that moment. I could not proceed with my fantasies as he robbed me out of the ground and threw me to a flowery fabric on top of my parents' bed. He left me for a few seconds to lock the door, and those few seconds felt like eternity without him, leaving me feeling cold and abandoned in some snowy desert.

"I can hear some footprints outside," he whispered as he untied his belt and I watched like a hawk, the smell of eros loud in m nostrils.. I observed his hips powerfully split up into a v-shape where his jeans laid unwillingly across them. My answer to his question or whatever statement he had made, was stuck in my throat, blocked by my watery mouth and longing soul. First experience could never feel so tempting. Noticing I was so numb, he laid on me, his fingers lingering throughout my whole body, forcing strangely beautiful lamentations out of my mouth.

"Jasmine! Are you in there?" My little sister's voice could be heard just across mom's room. If only she caught a glimpse of whatever game her holy sister was performing indoors, she could have been a saving grace. I was feeling drunk, intoxicated by wild feelings her precious voice could not redeem, I ignored her sounds and focused on Sydney who was staring at me, searching for my soul.

"Where could she be?" I heard my friend and classmate Cheryl's voice, who had an unquenchable crush for Sydney. "Maybe she's already at church; she could never miss this moment. You know how excited she is about her ordination." I overhead Jenny saying as she pulled and closed the door at our bedroom and they marched out.

"Damn me, I would've won him out today with this outfit. I really love Sydney with my soul." Cheryl said as their voices vanished on the sitting room after they closed the door. I let out a startled breath and kissed Sydney like he was the last thing I was allowed to kiss. I stripped off our clothes with so much swiftness that planted a stupor on his lust-filled face.

"Jay, need to go this far? I can always wait. I know you don't want this," he pleaded with me and I wondered why because his flesh was already dripping with beads of desirable sweat and his manhood was rock hard. I tossed and rolled burning with fever, I wanted everything he had to offer.

"Please Sydney," I begged.

"Your wish be my command."

He chopped my chastity as uncontrollable as the wave, as violent as the steam.

When I came back to my consciousness, my valuables had escaped my hand and flown to heaven-knows-where. I sat in bed, confused like a lost stranger, with a lump as bad as the itch on my throat. Sydney lay on top of the bed, his eyes mesmerizing me; mine could not encounter him, as I found him a man as greedy as a hog.

"I didn't know you adored me this much Jay, this is the best night of my life. I love you." I spit some huge amount of saliva on his face with heartfelt aversion. He wiped it away with a smile on his face, how could he not smile while he had been granted such importance? With tears streaming down my face I grabbed my bible which had been lying beside me during my evil game, and rushed towards the church with my aching body, waist and feet, the feeling was inexplicable, guilt, sorrow, regret and pain. What could be worse than a holy Mary's purity washed off that easily by the winds of the devil? What would the heavens say?

My mom's eyes were the first thing I collided with as I took one step toward the sacred place of God. She hurried towards me and held my hands with comfort; I stood like a statue and watched her and her unquestionable love towards me, tears now streaming down my soul. I cursed my birthday, cursed whoever thought I was worth it. I vowed to disagree with the ordination; I was stained and stinking, unfit no more to be called the leader or the servant of the Most High. I had to find a way to let them ordain a deserving sheep on my place.

"Baby, you got me worried! What took you so long? The prayer band is waiting for you."

"Mom, I don't think I can do this anymore," I said with a low voice.

"What? Why? What changed your mind? Where have you been? After all these preparations Jasmine, we don't want people mumbling?" mom lashed out at me. I could feel the super fear overtaking my energy.

"Jay! Thank God you've finally arrived! We've been searching for you everywhere. Come, the pastor is waiting for you." My dad dragged me by my hand before I could find answers to mom's raining questions and brought me in front of the pastor who introduced me to the congregation which shouted endless amen and gave hundred rounds of applause on my account. I faked a smile as I came in recognition that if I denied the ordination; I would break millions of hearts who were so happier and eager to have me as their leader. I had to take that risk and agree to the ordination. I saw my family smiling and waving at me and I smiled back with the most unbearable pain raining down my spine finding its way to my whole body and my soul, I had betrayed them severely but I had to keep it hidden. 'What they don't know won't kill them.' I thought. "Greetings to you all in the name of Jesus Christ." The pastor addressed the congregation.

"Amen!" Thousands of people from different branches and churches chanted.

"We were all waiting forward for this day and it has finally arrived. We're not God to judge but as the church we know who is capable of leading us without any form of trouble. We have trained and tested our young and committed member Jasmine; we see her fit to be the leader of the youths of our church. I hope we all know her; she is pure, chaste and exemplary to every child in this community and has inspired many people to start worshipping God. Jasmine has also agreed to serve God wholly and completely without any block in her way, meaning she'll stay here at church, serving God until she decides to get married. It's a strange thing to our church I know but if she feels that's her calling, why not offer her that chance? It's a beautiful thing, a very beautiful thing."

I rolled my mouth to both the sides and breathed heavily, a huge lump stood on my throat and I swallowed it but could not smile no more. I had to disagree with one idea of me staying at church; it would not be pleasant to.

"Jasmine, we'll have to first let you know that what you're doing is very strange to our church, we only agreed with you because we know that God communicates with each of us accordingly and we all have different callings. Secondly my daughter, you're standing in the pure ground, this is a sacred place, we're gathered with God and you know He's here right? God loves pure and honest souls, and making a vow with God is never ever easy to us fallible sinners, but if you do, make sure you're always in connection with Him. Therefore now I'll ask you some questions, you're taking your vows. Do you agree to give yourself wholly and completely to God?" the vow time began.

"Yes."

"Do you promise that you'll never do any vile thing, for example breaking your virginity outside marriage, just to serve your Almighty God?" I coughed a little bit as saliva blocked words on my throat.

"Y....Y....Yes pastor," 'mom save me please', I begged her with my eyes, I had wished that vow would never c... up with me, what were the angels saying in heaven about me?

"Do you agree that you will be an exemplary and fruitful leader to the youths and the church as a whole?"

"Yes"

Excitement rained down God's people as they clapped and praised while the devil's taunts heated my soul with overwhelming regret and inexplicable guilt.

"I am proud to also announce that she agreed to stay inside the church and will not stay with her family for God's purposes. Hence we will now ordain her to be a youth leader, a perfect leader, an offering to God"

"Amen!" I was absolutely still all the time, the moment of my immorality choking me to emotional death.

"Jasmine my daughter, May you be blessed amongst every daughter in this world, may you be the leader, a perfect and devoted leader of the youths. May every youth learn every good deed from you? Long live my daughter and bear the fruits of righteousness. We ordain you in front of God, to be the leader and we offer..."

"Pastor!" I broke the deafening silence in church and everybody glued their eyes on me as I held the pastor's hand when he was about to pour oil in my head. He stopped and gazed at me. Mom and dad were amazed and shocked too, but I had to stop him.

"I agree to be the youth leader and an offering to God, but don't pour this oil on my head and don't make me stay in church. I'll stay at home with mom and dad; this was a crazy idea really, pouring oils? We never do it in this church," I spoke calmly. I heard the rumblings and mumblings from the people but stood for myself and I read confusion on many people's faces including my parents.'

"All right daughter, that's no problem. I knew it was going to be hard for you to stay away from your parents. That's not a problem at all." He said as he stood up and prayed.

Everybody was surprised by my reluctance to have the oil poured on my head especially since I had had a huge bee on a bonnet about that night; it had been my own choice for heavens' sake. I reserved my fears for myself and worshipped the whole night with a lump sitting with a cap in my throat. The prayer band was on my case, praying so hard for me and I wept bitterly with them thinking, it was God's spirit essence within me and Him accepting me as an offering. I realized that Sydney had not returned back to church, it was a good idea because it would have been difficult for me to face the congregation while suffering from his glare. My family were the last ones to leave the church on Saturday after the ordination since the pastor was still praying for me. Mom, dad and aunt went before us after praising my holiness and encouraging my leadership skills, I followed behind with Jenny.

"Wow, congrats sis Jay, I'm walking with a new soul today. A supernatural spirit, I'm proud of you," she said as we slowly marched home.

"Thanks Jenny," I faked a smile, my mind was a million miles away.

"Is that all you have to say? You were over the moon about this ordination, what changed? You looked and sounded so dull all night. Are you alright sis?"

"I'm just a bit scared dear. I'm fine and I'm happy really, just a harmless anxiety."

"I understand sis, but relax, I bet it won't be that hard. You're used to these Godly things but why did you choose to stay home all of a sudden?"

"Weren't you going to miss me? Because I was already missing you and my family while standing in front of the whole congregation there," I said.

"I was really going to miss you, but I guess it's still fine you can work for God while staying with us," we both smiled and walked slowly towards home. To our surprise as we approached, mom and dad's sheets were washed and hanged on the washing line; I had that heartfelt gratitude for Sydney for his sensible thoughts. I cursed myself for ever forgetting all about mom's sheets, I had run carrying my lungs in my hands and forgot to destroy all evidence of my immorality behind. To silence all suspicion on everybody's mind, he had washed ours and aunt's too. Mom, aunt and dad standing on the washing line surprised by Sydney's behavior.

"Wow, what happened? You are one male chauvinist. You never do women chores, you always say washing is for women," aunt exclaimed, laughing and clapping hands for her only son, a beast of a son.

"I'm not that evil mom, I just thought of covering my sins," I threw him an owl eye and nearly lost consciousness.

"What sins now Sydney?" mom asked in confusion.

"I got caught up last night and could not see the angel's ordination, so I thought of doing something that might put a smile on everybody's face especially hers," he laughed and I exhaled loudly.

"Yeah you're clever. Otherwise I wasn't going to spare you. You missed the heavenly moment ever!" dad joined in on the conversation too as he and mom progressed indoors.

"Fill me on what happened uncle? What exactly did I miss?" he dried his hands with his trouser, moving towards my dad. I was watching his every move with disgust and pain.

"You're looking at our new youth leader; you're looking at a Godly woman. An ordained one of God!" Dad shouted with pride and determination.

"Wow, congrats beloved cousin! You deserve it!" he progressed towards me and tried shaking my hand but I pulled back and moved aside.

"What's wrong now Jasmine?" aunt asked wide eyed.

"Aunt he was supposed to be there but he wasn't," I lied, trying to fake a smile but failing.

"Oh my poor baby! Sorry, he said he got caught up. Forgive him okay?" mom comforted hugging me and I stood rigid, my eyes cursing Sydney.

"It's not a big issue. She's fine, just the fear I guess. Now let's go have breakfast I'm starving," dad said and Sydney smiled rudely at me.

I could not cover my shame and embarrassment; I ignored Sydney's eyes and rolled past him proceeding towards the bedroom. I watched mom and dad get into their room and nearly fainted with guilt. I had committed an unforgivable crime, worst part on their bed. Forgiving myself would never happen as long as I still had breathe. I disappeared in our room and wept, the ordination was just for making my parents happy else I would have spared it, I never deserved to be ordained. Sydney marched in as I was busy with regretting sobs. I furrowed my forehead in anger and stood up from bed making a disgusted face.

"You're the last thing I ever dream of seeing in front of me. You disgust me Sydney. I thought you were my cousin," I lashed out at him, trying hard to make sure my voice was low enough to only be heard by the two of us.

"Calm down Jay, I know you're hurting but you'll get used to it. Please don't cry..."

"Don't ask me to calm down stupid! You took my virginity and you're asking me to calm down, are you insane?" I nearly slapped him and he held my hand and squeezed it so tight. "If you raise your voice this damn high you'll draw attention to us. Let's sit down and talk about this calmly," he pulled me and tried sitting me on bed.

"I don't want to hear any word that comes out of your stinking mouth, so leave Sydney. Leave my father and my mother's compound and don't ever set your foot again here! I hate you with all I have. You tempted me, I should have gone back with that pastor's son but you blocked him knowing very well your intentions on me," I wept bitterly.

"Don't you ever try to pin this on me Jasmine? I asked you to stop at the kiss and you pulled me down! I gave you a chance but you were all over me. How is all this my fault now?" he warned.

"Just leave from here, you are the devil messenger dent to destroy me, just leave me alone."

"I don't want to lay my hand on you but you're slowly forcing me to," I saw his face turning red with anger and I stopped answering him back and continued sobbing. "If you need me, I'm here for you. I meant it that I love you but don't speak nonsense against me. I don't want to hurt you."

"Jasmine, Sydney! what's going on between you two?" dad barged into our house wearing an agitated face. I wiped off my tears and stared at the floor, searching for answers, wishing dad did not catch any word from our conversation. Sydney calmed down too and sat down on bed. "I'm talking to you both what's with this noise?"

"Jasmine is still mad at me for not attending her ordination uncle." he lied, knowing very well that dad was a no nonsense kind of man.

"I thought we spoke about this matter a few minutes back and settled it, why are you making a big deal out of this Jasmine?" my dad asked in annoyance.

"I...I didn't mean to dad, it's just that, he had promised to be there." I searched for sensible lies but could not find it, my heart was bleeding. The whole family barged in and stood at the door. "Is there more to it? Why is Jasmine crying? You want to tell us something we don't know?" dad asked while everybody kept quiet and stared at us, the victims.

"Uncle, I've already said my piece, this matter overheated until I nearly raised my hand on her that's why she's crying. She' just being dramatic for no reason," Sydney said as he stood up and headed towards the door, dad blocked his way out. "You're not going anywhere until you tell us what's going on! Jasmine what's wrong? It's not three hours after your ordination and you're already fighting. You want to embarrass us? This behavior must stop now!"

"This will stop dad, but it's either I leave this house today or Sydney leaves! I think there are demons using this guy," I stood up, wiped my tears and spoke with determination while throwing owl's eyes at Sydney.

"What?" aunt screamed.

"Wait Jay! What's wrong with you all of a sudden?" Jenny marched towards me and held my hands, stared at my eyes searching for hidden answers.

"Jasmine baby! What happened?" Mom begged me to go back to my senses. I realized I was about to betray myself and sat down shedding tears.

"I will leave! I'll never come back here," Sydney said as he pulled his suitcase out of the wardrobe and tried marching out. Everybody's face wore confusion and anger towards me. "You're not going anywhere Sydney!" aunt roared and pulled the suitcase from Sydney and placed it back on the wardrobe, however Sydney went out quietly.

"He's my beloved cousin, he promised to be there at my ordination but he didn't show up. I wanted him so bad to be a Christian like me but he turned me down. Now that I'm asking him the reason why, he wants to slap me. Why aunt why? I love him, he is my cousin, and how could he do that to me, me his beloved cousin?" I wept bitterly; weeping for my lost chastity and making them believe something else. Dad came and rubbed my back and everybody's face calmed down, I awarded myself a trophy for acting well.

"Calm down baby girl, he has already apologized for his absence. He will be fine; it takes time dragging someone to God. He'll end up a Christian someday okay? Just calm down for your father who loves you lots and forgive your cousin. He loves you Baby and we all know he wouldn't have missed out if he wasn't surely caught up"

"I will forgive him dad, I promise. Maybe its God's spirit working inside of me already and it's against Sydney." I faked a smile and everybody laughed, I was however glad that they finally believed me and they took their ways back to the kitchen and left me sitting on bed with a bleeding heart. I realized how much my family loved me, I never wanted to imagine to what state their hearts would be after learning out mine and Sydney's story.

I felt so empty and useless without my virginity, it was my pride and the most valuable thing I had with me. It was really hard believing it was no longer with me and was no longer coming back to me. I had vowed to keep it until marriage and mom and aunt were very proud of me that unlike Janet, I was so determined to stay pure. However that day I saw Janet far much better than me because even if she was not a virgin, she had never slept with her cousin and she was never shy to say she was sexual active, her life was not so much private, and she had nothing to hide. My life was going to be a nightmare from then because everything I was going to see was going to remind me I was no longer pure and I lost my purity on my parents' bed. I remembered how I always laughed at my friends for giving away it away to boys before marriage. I wondered where my faith and love for God had been during my evil actions, I had fallen so easily to a temptation and it was slowly eating me away. My day was dull and horrible and I was totally failing to fake my happiness. I started to hate myself for the person I had become, how could I be so weak? Where was the part of me that loved God and prayed? I was eating away, what could be worse than having a prayer warrior's chastity washed off so easily by the winds of the devil. I slept, without having food or bathing, they tried making me eat but I faked illness.

Next morning I woke up so early and I started cleaning up slowly and prepared breakfast. I heated water for mom who had to go to church since it was Saturday. Staring at my mom, the wound deepened. How would she feel if she knew that her Mary was no longer Mary but Jezebel? She had raised me with so much love and respect; she had warned me in every area about losing my virginity. Mom believed in me and wanted the best for me. By giving Sydney my body, I had given away myself to him. I assured myself I was safe because it was only me and Sydney who knew about the secret. I sat on the couch and did not move, in case mom noticed something fishy.
****

Because of increasing pressure those days, Sydney left before his time; he could not bear my hatred no more. I made sure I avoided him so severely that everybody noticed and I openly showcased my anger towards him. I convinced my family that

God's spirit was working on me and was against Sydney and his behaviors since I was ordained. They believed it without thinking twice and had tried to make Sydney worship but to no avail.

He never visited us since that day. I tried every day to come to terms with my broken virginity and made sure I led the church very well, everybody still believed I was pure and chaste and it was awesome for me to keep it that way. I had received my ordinary level results and had passed; hence I went and did my advanced level. Sadly, my father passed on the following year when I was doing my first year in advanced level, form five. He succumbed to some heart disease, even though it was eating me every day that my father had died without me telling him the truth, I was glad somehow that I had managed to keep him happy all the days of his life. I was still considered a prayer warrior at my church and was glad to have moved past all the incidences, I had tried forgetting about all my shenanigans and focused on my duties and my education. I had vowed to make up for my mistakes by taking good care of my mother since she had lost her husband. I finished my advanced level and passed with flying colors too, it was exciting to me, to my mom and to every church member to see me excel in life that way.

CHAPTER THREE

One windy and cloudy evening, mom was humming church songs inside her bedroom, I was slicing tomatoes in the kitchen preparing supper and Janet was lying on the couch wearing a vest and a bum short busy receiving and sending WhatsApp texts to her friends and boyfriends. She never did let me take a glance at her mobile phone but I could tell by the way her lips would curve every time she read messages that whatever topic she was discussing with her friends was wild. I had finished my advanced level and taking a gap year while mom was trying to make funds meet so as to let me proceed to varsity. Jenny was in form three by then.

"Won't you come and help me prepare supper Jenny?" I begged.

"Sis please, be merciful to me," she wasn't even looking at me.

"Tomorrow the dishes are yours ma'am, don't ever call me for assistance..." I was interrupted by mom's mobile phone ringing and Janet ignoring it.

"Don't tell me you can't hear mom's phone ringing Jenny?" I shouted.

"Might be mom's boring friends asking about money for clubs and blah," she was not even staring at me, busy smiling at her phone.

"Go give it to her then Jenny!" I roared.

"Sis please, I'm having better conversations here. You go give her yourself."

I jumped from the kitchen and grabbed mom's phone seeing Jenny was solid in her statements and was never going to move. It was Aunt Maggie and instead of rushing to mom's bedroom to hand over her phone, I responded to it.

"Aunty, hello," my lips curved in a gentle smile.

"Jay baby! how are you?" I could sense relief in her voice that it was me who had answered the phone.

"I'm alright aunt and everyone is alright," I giggled.

"Won't you ask me how is your cousin doing?"

"I was just about to ask. How's he?" I bit my lower lip cringing, aunt knew I and Sydney had become water and oil, the mention of his name awoken some bile in my tongue.

"He's alright. He'll be holidaying with you guys since he's done with his varsity and awaiting graduation." She said in ecstasy kind of waiting for me to react.

"Oh!" I wished the earth could swallow me, Sydney's countenance was the last thing I was dreaming of meeting. He was the worst page to my book, I had healed and moved on with life but there he was, to open my old wounds.

"Jay but why? I suggested he come over there maybe you guys will try and get along. If you hate my son it hurts me you know that. If you don't want him to come over tell me so," aunt growled.

"I don't have a problem really aunt. He may come if he wants to," I said with a low tone, trying hard to sound calm.

"Sydney loves you Jay, a lot. He wishes all these games would stop. What kind of life are we going to live if we hate each other as a family?"

"Sydney can come if he wants to aunt but…" I swallowed some words.

"There's more to this story right?"

"No aunt, it's alright. I'm happy that my cousin is coming over, we are all happy." I hung up and closed my eyes for a minute and caught Janet starring at me with confuse "Stop giving me that look, why are you giving me that look?" I said as I slowly dragged myself to sit and leaned my head on my hands, tears filling my eyes.

"what's wrong? What did aunt say?"

"That evil man is coming for holidays. I don't want to catch a glimpse of him. I will have to find another place to stay," I said, swallowing the tears and the lump that stood on my throat. Jenny widened her eyes, trying hard to understand.

"And by evil man you mean Sydney?" she asked in shocked giggle.

"Jay, you say the reason you hate Sydney this much is only because he didn't attend your special night? Or that God's spirit doesn't love his lifestyle? I personally think you are not being fair," I knew Jenny wanted to use her intelligence on me. I did not reply to that question. "I think the same spirit of God same one that teaches us to love and forgive one another and to also not judge."

"I don't know if ever in this lifetime I will be able to forgive Sydney for what he did to me, any sane person would hold such a grudge." I swore within me, anger rising in my veins as I thought about the events of that night.

"Jasmine sis, what did Sydney do to you? Did he rape you maybe? You can't hold a grudge to such a silly matter as someone not attending your day that's ridiculous. You are lying sis and I'm not used to you doing that. I think you're hiding something and you know very well that I will find out," I nearly choked myself when I heard Jenny talking about finding out why. I realized I had shown too much emotions and I was slowly betraying myself.

"No Jenny! Rape, why would you think something so horrible. I have multiple reasons why I don't get along with Sydney. I liked that pastor's son you guys found me with. He could be a perfect match for me since I'm Godly, but Sydney provoked him and he left, I've never seen him since that day." Jenny would stop her nonsense of digging deep on my affairs.

"Oh I see." Jenny laughed but I could still see she kind of did not believe it.

"I always knew there was too much to this. Don't worry my love, if you want to hook up with that pastor's son, I will find connections you know me very well and please forget about the ordination, it happened two years back for heaven's sake you should have chilled by now. Forgive him sis please."

"It's my everyday prayer Jenny," I faked a smile.

I stood up and headed towards mom's bedroom and shared the news with her.

"It's been long since he last visited us Jay. I did not see him during your dad's burial; I heard he went back the same day," she said while cleaning her room.

"Yeah mom," that was all I had to say.

"Mmmm, my lovely daughter let me give you an advice, come and sit here and help me with these blankets," I went and sat next to her.

"Jay my love, you were ordained to be a leader and that's just because they saw leadership skills in you. If you as a leader could despise someone this bitterly, what do you expect others to do? They will think it's the right thing to do. Sydney is your cousin and he apologized for not coming to your ordination which I believe is the sole reason why you hate him. Forgive people and your life will be easier. God won't bless you if you keep on with this, let it go and lead the flock the right way." Mom was preaching and I listened attentively, if only she knew the depth of the story.

"I understand mom, I'm trying. I will get there maybe."

"That's my daughter, but that's vile remember and you vowed to God not to ever commit any vile crime. God punishes people who won't keep their vows sweetheart, never vow if you're not ready to keep them."

"Mom, that sheet is too old why don't you get rid of it?" I had caught a glimpse of the same sheet on which Sydney had destroyed my life and I started shaking and beads of sweat formed on my skin.

"I love this sheet baby; I will never throw it away." Mom laughed as she cherished the sheet and smelled it, her face displaying the sweetness of the memories that ran in her head.

"Your dad loved it so much, it's the first sheet he bought for our bed and I have so many sweet memories when I look at it. It's the sheet that has my life in it. I respect it, I love it. It reminds me of your father every time I see it. It's our oldest sheet and we both were fond of it, the first tool in our marriage after our wedding," she chuckled while shedding a tear. I could not hold mine either, it came as a good opportunity that hers were shed otherwise mine were going to betray me. I rubbed her back and kissed her cheek.

"It's okay mom. May his precious soul rest in peace," I noticed again, that the crime I had committed two years back was unforgivable. I was scared of praying, I did not know how I was going to address the matter to God. Shaking with fear, I went out and wept my soul out on our own bedroom. That was my reaction every time Sydney's name was brought to life. Jenny finished the cooking as she saw I was no longer ready for the kitchen that day. I had promised myself, especially after my father's death that I was going to be my mother's strength and comfort. I was failing to be all that because of my miseries.

I had become too clingy and too close to her until her friends and my friends started complaining and mom herself thought she was the one being overprotective with me while it was the other way round. Whenever guilty conscience takes hold of you, it controls you, how you think, what you say and how you react.

"You should let her go and be free with the outside world Laurie; she will learn a lot of things in life and won't give you any problems," one colleague of my mom had told her one day when I visited her workplace.

"I'm not sure about that dear, look at Janet, I let her go thinking her behavior would transform but she has gotten even worse," mom had said with a worried look, with her milky white uniform fitting on her like a glove. I hated seeing that look on her face though.

"I get that, my friend, but remember she has to explore what's out there so that it won't be difficult for her in the near future," she advised.

Later that night mom called me to her bedroom and begged me to make friends.

"Jay I understood well what Sister Rose meant, I felt guilty really, that I'm protecting you too much beyond your wishes. I think it's time you choose your own friends but make sure you don't choose friends that will influence you to bad habits," she begged, holding my hand and pressing it softly.

"Don't worry much about me mom, I promised to never hurt you. You're my friend and you're enough for me. I see a lot of things on Television and I learn every day. I also do have a few friends from school, Cheryl and Mercy, I might not see them everyday but I see them from time to time and that's enough," I convinced her. I felt so bad to see my mother in that condition, feeling like she was imprisoning me.

"It's okay baby, as long as you're comfortable with it. I don't want you to think I'm the one who doesn't want to see you out in the world," she laughed and hugged me.

I had a few friends whom I constantly stayed in touch with. My closest friends were Cheryl and Mercy who were my former classmates. They were not much of church people even though they went almost every Saturdays with me. They went there just to please me, or at least that was what they told me. Cheryl, we were a bit close but we did not spend time together as I was always indoors and communication was not easy between us since I had no cell phone. She had became a friend to Janet too and more Janet's friend than mine. Cheryl was into boys like Janet but I never judged her as we were friends, however I always tried preaching to her to leave her sinful ways. Our characters conflicted as we were not compatible to each other. She liked me a lot though for my kind behavior. Mom had thought Cheryl was a bad influence to me but I had convinced that I would not succumb to the ravages of peer pressure; she however still did not like her for a fleet of boyfriends she had and also married men. Cheryl was known by the whole community to be a home wrecker and a girl who would do anything for money. Cheryl had undying lust for Sydney, she would hunt him down every time he visited us but he would just ignore her. Janet had tried hooking them up but to no avail; I did not support Jenny on her idea as I thought Sydney and Cheryl were not going to work.

Mercy on the other hand was a free soul and we got along very well. She had only one boyfriend from school and she was not a prostitute, mom liked her. We had a special connection with each other and we visited each other gradually and we shared a lot of things, her mom liked me a lot and had become my mother's friend because of me. Communication with my friends was not easy because I had no cell phone. Mom had asked if she could buy me one and I had rejected the offer. I just wanted to convince her I was her pure girl and she was convinced and she loved it.

****

Janet washed the dishes after supper and I got busy with tiding up the house in preparation of Sydney's arrival which would be a worst nightmare to me. Mom was busy pinning her patients' files in her bedroom and Janet started dressing up, I could tell she was going for a sleep over. I held the broom with one hand,

"And you? Where are you heading to so late?"

"There'll be more of this for the following days Jay, maybe for the rest of this holiday," she said, buttoning up her jeans and pulling her blue sneakers from under the bed.

"What are you talking about? How do you think mom feels about your behavior? How could you just sneak out like this Jenny you're too young for this," I pleaded, trying to lower my voice so mom could not hear our conversation.

"I'm 16 now Jay, I don't need anyone's consent to make my own decisions. Everybody at my age does this; you didn't do it because you're God's child. So let me be....."

"You're not going anywhere today Janet!" mom hissed. I had not recognized her; I did not know how long she had been standing there.

"Sorry mom! But you won't stop me from doing this. I heard Sydney will be visiting you guys over here and I'm too old to sleep on the couch. I'll be better off at my friend's," she said rudely. My heart boiled with anger, I wished I could throw a hard slap at her but held myself. I looked at my mom, she looked at her with teary eyes, and her face wore surrender. I could imagine how she felt, blasphemed by the fruit of her womb, she felt like she had failed as a mother. She stood there like a statue with tears flooding down her cheeks. Janet hurried past my mom like a whirlwind, swinging her bag rudely, banged the door on us and disappeared. I sat my mom on our bed and hugged her. If my secret blew out of the closet, mom was going to indeed feel like a failure as a mother. Both of her daughters were just rotten eggs.

"It's okay mom, I'm here for you," I comforted, rubbing her back softly.

"I had forgotten that you're my pill Jay. I still got you.." I was amazed to see mom smiling again. I smiled back with teary eyes and we ended up laughing together. I surely was my mom's pain reliever; joy would fill her heart as soon as she remembered me. I escorted her to her bedroom and made sure she slept well.

"Goodnight mom, I love you..." I said, kissing her forehead and glad I was still able to make her happy despite every vile thing I kept inside of me.

"I love you even more baby," she beamed and pulled the blankets to her face. I hesitated to move for a split second enjoying being my mother's beloved and trusted one. I went and resumed with my cleaning process.

****

The day our cousin was expected to visit arrived. It was Thursday and I was with mom, preparing scones for breakfast, Janet had not returned from where she had gone. Mom was by my side making tea and we were chatting about how she was going to be late for work when her phone rang. I went and received it.

"...are you related to a Sydney Dawns?" the man on the call asked as I had just received the call.

"Yes I am, he's my cousin."

"Is there any elder person near you there?" I handed the phone over to my mom.

"Yes, yes I know him. What????" mom dropped the phone on the floor and held her head with both her hands. She stood rigid and could not move. Her eyes wide open. I died with both curiosity and panic. Something was wrong with my cousin, I thought.

"Mom what's wrong?" I asked breathing heavily. Mom tried to speak but the words would not come out of her mouth. I stood there running up and down like an idiot, feeling like calling the neighbors but could not know what I would say to them. "Baby, I need to go. You remain behind and take care of everything in the house," finally words managed to come out of her mouth even though she was still trembling and shaking. She rushed to her bedroom, grabbed her handbag. I waited for her at the door betting to block her way until she told me what was wrong.

"Mom what is wrong?" there was both begging and annoyance in my voice. I needed to know what was wrong but she was ignoring me. I blocked the door so she could not pass through without letting me know what had been said on the phone. She gave up, seeing I was not going to leave the doorway until she told me what was wrong.

"Your cousin had an accident after he landed, he has been rushed to the hospital, I'm going there I'll let you know how he is when I get back," her voice sunk in her throat; she gave me a last glance and went out. I stood there lifeless and dumb.

I looked at everything and nothing made sense. I saw what the pastor had told us at church making sense, that we should learn to forgive people when they alive. My worst fear caught me, what if he died? God was going to be angry with me. I threw myself to the couch and threw myself on it so severely that I felt the pain on my waist. Tears fell unwelcomed, there was only one solution for me; prayer, which I did a lot. I needed to be with someone because the pain was so unbearable for me alone, unfortunately Janet was not there and mom had left with her phone and there was nobody to update me on his condition. I needed to mend ties with him before he died; it was never going to be a walk in the park. Why did I still need him after what he did to me? After a long period of time, mom arrived and told me that Sydney was in a bad condition but he was going to be alright.

His mother, Aunt Maggie had arrived and was with him in the hospital. Mom had come home to collect some few necessities needed for him and she was going back to the hospital. She went back and I was left alone again in the house till late at night, the amount of tears I shed amazed me. My head was spinning and I thought of him whole day. I was caught between the devil and the evil storm. Janet arrived and she was so drunk, I tried sharing the sad news with her but she would not listen to me. So I gave up and spent my night praying and crying.

"What's with Sydney Jay? You pray we all know, but you never pray this damn much! C'mon bro, God has heard you. I want to sleep you disturbing me and besides, you're praying for a nigga that will come and you'll ignore him like he's a piece of rubbish. We didn't plant this hatred for him in your heart, you should've apologized back then to him, you're starting to annoy me," Janet roared at me by night as I was busy sobbing and praying out loud.

Friday and Saturday passed and mom and Aunt were still there with Sydney at the hospital. I was dying with impatience. Janet heard the news when she became sober but she did not seem to care as much as I did and I had given up on trying to make her understand. She was way too busy with her wild life.

"Sydney is a handsome dude; handsome dudes like him never die. He must come home and I'll find a pretty girl for him. I have my pretty friends. Tell him to recover speedily sis Jay, Cheryl smacks him a lot," Janet had said as I left on Sunday to the hospital to see my cousin. I ignored her and went out, wearing my linen dress which was simple and respectful but I knew, judging from the huge mirror on our bathroom, that I looked good and natural. I was so comfortable with my looks despite seeing Janet painting herself with makeup every day. I was annoyed by my little sister who only thought of finding a girl for a person who was not expected to come out of the hospital bed alive.

As slowly as a tortoise, I entered the ward where he was admitted and there was mom and Aunt looking sick themselves. I shifted my eyes towards the bed where my lovely cousin was lying and some fiery pained hit me hard. His head was covered with bandages and he lied lifeless and that made despair glue to my mind like a sticky tape. I knelt down near the bed and recited a prayer because that was the only thing I could help with. I greeted my aunt and she replied me with tears. I understood. Mom and aunt were dirty and sleepy, they needed some rest. As I was busy with my sad thoughts, the blankets shook and we all stood in relief.

CHAPTER FOUR

I was awakened by a tall, brown-skinned and brawny male nurse whose face resembled somebody I knew even though I could not remember who it was. That was when I realized I had fallen asleep on a chair while praying the previous night. I stretched myself, yawned and stood up.

"Sorry dear, I need to use the bathroom, am I allowed using this one?" I asked sincerely pointing to the bathroom that was located inside Sydney's ward.

"No, come here. I'll show you the right place" He said with his lips curving in a marvellous smile.

"Just go along this corridor, this last door is the main bathroom for people who are taking care of their patients" He pointed the place to me and I thanked. I was still trying to remember who he was, because he looked so familiar.

"I'm Travis; you may call me anytime if you need anything."

"I think I know you from somewhere?"

"Yes, from church." He laughed gentle with his Michael Jordan's brown eyes lightening. He was the same guy I had met during the night of my ordination, our church pastor's son. I never knew he was a nurse, I would see him at church during school holidays, proving he had been schooling in some fancy and expensive schools since he had financially stable parents.

"That's right." A smile radiated though my face as I admired his kindness and feeling guilty for having been bitter towards him during that night because of Sydney.

"You looked different by then."

"I know right, I was young and beardless and no muscles, I was a young boy by then I'm a man now." He laughed gentle.

"Understood really," I joined him in laughter.

"I've got to go." I strolled past him and went in search of a place to bath.

I came back from the bathroom with an expectation to find mom and Aunt Maggie on the ward but they were absent and I knew their plan for me to bond with my cousin was serious to an extent of them giving us space. I bumped with Travis again on the doorway and he gazed at me with total reverence as he blocked my way in.

"I know you as Jay because that's how I hear your parents call you, what's your full name you never told me your name back then, you were a hard nut to crack," he chuckled.

"Oh I'm Jasmine."

"Your name is as beautiful as you Jasmine. I'd be overjoyed if I had your phone number, mind sharing?" He pulled out a cell phone from his pocket and stretched his hand to hand it over to me.

"I'm sorry, I don't own a cell phone," I said with a calm face and his forehead furrowed in some gentle disbelief as he placed his phone back on his pocket.

"Your cousin is awake and in a better state now. He's still weak though but I believe he'll be totally well by the end of the day. I believe it's your prayers that healed him."

"What do you mean my prayers?" I asked in total confusion. "I heard you praying last night and I could judge by those prayers how much of a good girl you are. You're still what I liked from day one" I gave him a bitter sweet look and shifted my attention towards my cousin; I needed Travis as nothing more than a mere buddy, no love talk.

Sydney's eyes were wide open and he was staring at me. He was still pale and was breathing slowly, the oxygen machine was no longer on his nose and he looked better than the previous day and some bruises had healed and bandages removed. Travis left the room after noticing I was a million miles away from him; my attention was with my cousin. Looking at his face just ignited a spark of memories in my head that fuelled my anger towards him. I exhaled loudly as I sat on the chair beside the bed.

"Since when do you care?" He broke the silence I wish I had broken with his low pale voice but still thick and beautiful; I rolled my eyes at the realization that he was still arrogant even in his death bed.

"You were dying I had to see you..." I breathed deeply trying hard to control my raging anger. "How are you feeling now?" I proceeded.

"I can see right through you Jasmine, one thing you'll never succeed with me is faking that damn kindness, you can go if you don't feel like being here with me because I know you don't want to" He spoke with a harshly pale voice and I closed my eyes tightly trying hard to avoid an evil feeling that nearly made me slap his cheek.

"You're right. I don't want to be here Sydney; I did it because mom and aunt want me to." I responded rudely.

"I wonder how they'll feel once they learn about the truth." He smiled wickedly and bit his lower lip.

"Is that a threat?" My heart reached a boiling point and I let out a hot breath.

"I don't do threats honey, I just don't know how your family will feel if they come to know that every action and every word, every promise that come out of your mouth is unreal." I rushed towards him like an annoyed chicken, swearing and boiling.

"I'll strangle you I swear."

"Stop this damn act or I'll crack your bones Jay! Boil down to your senses!" He woke up and gripped both my hands so tight in aggravation. I blinked harder and shed an angry tear as our eyes swore at each other in total displeasure.

"Don't you ever dare talk to me like that Sydney; you're the reason behind my fake behavior if there be such. I wouldn't be doing all this if you had never taken my virginity." Sharp pains attacked my soul as I spoke of my lost virginity, one thing I had vowed to never lose; I remembered Janet's words that she had whispered to me the day before my ordination.

"I did not force you Jasmine! I didn't hold you at gunpoint! We both felt like it. You consented to it." I forcefully pulled my hands off him and held my waist.

"I wouldn't have done it if you hadn't gone home with me. How could I have known your intentions? You made me fall for you."

"Find the damn solutions and stop filling my damn brains with flipping blame!" He scolded and I moved back with fear. Tears still filled my eyes and I sat on my chair feeling defeated, Sydney was never a soft rock.

"Don't ever dare come back here if you're going to be acting like a toddler Jay, be mature and it's going to be easy dealing with you." He finished his sentence with a warning.

"Do you know what my virginity meant to me? It was my life Sydney! My passport to marriage." I said in painful sobs. "You're acting a flipping movie. Who said non-virgins don't marry?" He mocked.

"You won't understand I know and the worst part is, my own cousin took my virginity, that's insane."

"Cousins marry these days, nothing surprising about that." He spoke vilely and I wiped my tears realizing he was never going to understand my anger.

"So tell me, for how long will you pretend to be holy?"

"That's none of your business, God still love me despite of my flaws, and I apologized to Him."

"I see but I think forgiving you was going to be easy if you didn't cover sin with another sin of hating on me."

"Go to hell! I'll never forgive you Sydney! I'll never do it." I swore.

"Fine then, what's your solution to this? I'll take anything because I don't give a damn about you and your prickling moods."

"Let's pretend to be cool with each other in front of our family." I said in determination, knowing very well if I made things look very well in front of my family nothing was going to prickle.

"I'm not so good with pretending, I'm not fake." He scorned.

"Then what the hell do you want Sydney?"

"Go to hell and report yourself missing, nagging little caterpillar!"

"Sydney! What is all this?" We noticed Aunt Maggie and mom standing on the door way with their hands on their mouths. Sydney laughed out louder and I stared at him confused a little, he winked an eye at me and I laughed too, getting to terms with his signs.

"What mom? Jay is tripping; she keeps on annoying me about bathing thrice a day like I'm a teenage girl. I'm telling her where to get off." Sydney fought a good battle. I saw the skins on their foreheads unfolding up and they laughed.

"Oh good! Glad now that everything is fine. I thought you guys were still fighting." Aunt said as she hugged her son and kissed his cheeks.

I could sense a whirlwind of joy hallucinating her as she jumped up and down screaming after noticing her son's quick recovery. She started her favorite church song and danced as mom joined her along and we all clapped and laughed. Sydney could not help but flash his milky white teeth and I suddenly felt my anger washing away. I kind of started feeling like I was wasting my time on worrying about what they would say, they loved me. I was safe and was still worshipping God.

"The prayer of a righteous man has all the power to raise the sick from his sickbed." I whispered with a glowing face. Everyone laughed and mom gazed at me with a look of love that told me everything I needed to know.

"Indeed! The angels are singing in heaven I'm sure today." I felt the comfort of a mother's love in her bosom as she passed a warm hug to me, a perfect place for every child to be.

"I've always loved and trusted you completely, I always will my little Jay." Aunt said smiling in tears.

"I'm also glad that she and her cousin buried the hatchet! Her leadership skills are finally showing through, I'm the happiest woman alive." Exclaimed mom. Seeing her that happy was my goal in my everyday life.

"I'm sure my team at church miss me a lot mom. Imagine no Bible study group for three full days!" I smiled.

"They do baby! But Travis teaches them these days, he's a great preacher too and they all enjoy the lessons with him too."

Mom knew Travis; he was one devoted church member, loved by the church too for his peculiar behavior.

"Oh that's great mom. I'm no longer stressed now, I was worried for them."

"I guess now that we're here you can go home and rest, you may even go and check on your team at once and ask for prayers." She handed me the keys and I stretched my arms to take them, Sydney pulled my hand back.

"No aunt, Jay will pray over here if she needs to pray. I need her with me here." My eyes widened in confusion, Sydney would have paid a million dollar to a person who had to throw me out of his ward, and I wondered what had changed his mind suddenly.

"Oh! Really?" Mom was also confused and caught in disbelief. "Heaven knows how happy I am to see my two favorite people in the world uniting!" Aunt shed a tear and hugged both of us at the same time.

"You may stay behind Jay; all I need is to see you guys happy together."

"Take care of him then dear, we'll have to leave now. We just can't miss Travis' sermons." They said as they stood up to leave.

"Okay mom, I'll do so. Don't forget to tell my group that I miss being with them, telling them about God."

"I won't forget honey." Mom kissed my cheek and I waved as they left.

"Well done with this one." I said as I turned back to look at Sydney.

"I'm not as dumb as you; all you saw fit was opening the eyes wider and faking smiles." He grabbed his blankets and tried to sleep without having the bed down on the right level.

"You still need my help with that." I stood up, ignoring the pride in his face and winded the bed down. I shook my head and went back to my chair, pulled my blankets to my face and faded off to sleep.

****

I stayed another two full days at the hospital and Travis made sure I got everything I needed, from food, a place to sleep, clothes and cell phones for communicating with my family about Sydney's condition. He was also updating me about how my group was doing at church. We held Bible study groups every afternoon by two to four o'clock. I was the one who had reinforced that habit since it had been long forsaken at the church. The pastor and the elders were overjoyed by all the hard work and the sleepless nights I spent working for my God. The number of attendants had increased from day one, youths and other young people from different churches came to listen to my teachings. They were my motivation and teaching them about anything from God, love, sex and life inspired me a lot. They saw me as an exemplary young girl, even my friends from school usually came too. I missed them a lot when I chose staying with Sydney at the hospital but for the sake of covering my secret up I had to sacrifice all that.

After those two days, Sydney had gained his strength; he could walk slowly, he could bath and eat by himself, we did not talk that much, I just made sure he had his medication, had bathed and was well fed and I never ceased praying for him. It was a great relief for me that we were both trying hard to ignore our anger towards each other and be cousins and forget about our mating and I was feeling like everything was going back to normal.

Janet came to visit us on the second day and she could not keep quiet about finding my cousin a girlfriend and I would go mad at her every time she mentioned it but after dwelling for long on the matter, I saw it would be a good idea for us to find Sydney a girlfriend at our area. She would make me forget totally about him.

"Jay. You're always at church day and night. He needs a girl to soothe him, he's been sick for long." Jenny said on the second day as we sat on the floor with Sydney.

"But you're right Jenny, Sydney needs a woman." I held my chin with my hand thoughtfully

"Stop this nonsense you two brats. It's funny that you talking about me as if I'm not there. If I need a girl I'll find her myself" Sydney scolded us as Travis approached the room and there was an awkward silence amongst us.

"Relax *Cuz*; we know exactly what's good for you. I have somebody in mind." She smiled and nodded her head thoughtfully, "Cheryl, your best friend, you know she always had a thing for Sydney."

"Yeah, great idea." I said, shaking uncomfortably.

"Big booty? Big boobs? Because I could do with only that?" Sydney mocked.

"Love is not about boobs and booty! Love is different. But relax, she has all that." I smiled, thinking how happy Cheryl was going to be after hooking her up with Sydney.

"Fine, my stay here is going to be a bit longer I guess and I can't do without a girl soothing me."

"We knew that right?" Jenny said as she picked the phone and dialled Cheryl's number. Sydney was staring at me and I exhaled louder with a little frown on my face.

"Are you fine Jay?"

"Why wouldn't I be? I'm okay"

"Great then!"

"Yeah, I've spoken to Cheryl; she agreed to visit here anytime soon. I'm pretty sure she'll be here soon. The game is played now everything is good." Jenny interrupted the awkwardness as I smiled and nodded my head. Sydney stayed quiet.

"Jasmine, I've been looking for you all over the place." Travis interrupted the silence in the room with his syrupy voice.

"You knew I was here, didn't you?" I reddened with blushing, just to convince Sydney that I was moving on from the hurt, and I stood up. The face Janet wore made me laugh, it was her first time seeing me talking to a male person other than my friends from school and I knew it made her more excited and more curious at the same time. I ignored her and went straight to Travis who hugged me a bit longer than I had expected and I closed my eyes, not admiring him or his hearty hug. Janet could not stop winking her eye at me and biting her lower lip in enthusiasm. It was high time I convinced her I was falling in love with somebody because I knew it was going to awkward with Sydney under our roof, I did not have feelings for Travis but I had to smile and pretend they were there.

"Your cousin will be discharged the day after tomorrow. I don't think your mom will be coming over anymore, she said so on the phone." He spoke with his rough voice.

"Ohh! Okay. Thank you for letting us know." I smiled. "It's okay. May I please talk to you for a moment?" He walked out slowly, waiting for me to follow him.

"Fine. I'm right behind you" I said reluctant to go but I knew very well that if I had refused, Janet was going to laugh at me for the whole week. So I shifted my attention towards her as she pulled my hand and brought me aside for a 'talk'.

"Oh he's cute *bruh*, Travis! So that's him?" She shouted, smiling nonstop in total disbelief.

"So Jay he's the reason you don't wanna stay home these days. I heard mom saying you refused to go back home. So now I see, my sister is in love and that with the guy mom would be happy to see you with!" She jumped up and down like a puppy.

"Shut up Jenny!" I interrupted her. Sydney was staring at me with kind of disgusted eyes, kind of believing that Travis was the reason why I never wanted to go home not him. "You're too forward; I'm not yet in love with him"

"I wasn't born yesterday; I know chemistry when I see it. You guys connect. What do you say Syd?" Sydney ignored the question and looked away. Janet winked her eye at me and kissed my cheek.

"Go now Jay. Please make sure you entertain this nigga, this is your only way to happiness, you've lived a lonely life for long sister now grab this opportunity. Don't act too serious or boring. Get your chill. Take as much time as you want." That was exactly like Janet. She said pushing me to the door and I nearly fell down laughing at the way she was overjoyed. I turned around to look at Travis.

"Please don't take too long I need to...."

"Relax Jay," He interrupted me. He held both my hands and looked at me straight in the eyes.

"I'm sure you can say whatever you wanna say without holding my hands Trav?" Trav was the shortcut I heard from his friends and had started preferring it instead of Travis. As if he had not captured what I had just said, he grabbed me again by my hands and gazed at me.

"I'm sorry, I like holding hands with people I love too much but yeah I guess your wish is my command." He let go of my hands and just got lost in my eyes as if lost in some Garden of Eden, I felt a little uncomfortable.

"Well, I just want to be friends with you, to get to know you better to..." "Trav I..."

"I'm just letting you know that you've been bossing the orchards of my heart lately, seeing you everyday here just brings a smile to my face. You're some different woman. I never forgot you since I saw you that night at church, the night of your ordination and those few weekends I got to see you at church during my short holidays. It's so perfect seeing a woman choose God whilst others get busy with the world you know."

I was clueless on what to say and how to react but the name 'ordination' just caused me a severe panic attack remembering that if I had had gone back with him; I would still have had my virginity with me. Travis was the kind of guy every church girl would have loved being involved them with. He was every church girl's crush, for his handsome face; even though not as handsome as Sydney, for his voice when talking or singing and his sermons as he preached. He was a Godly man.

"I don't really have a problem being your friend. I would be glad having a friend like you." Deep down within me there was no feeling for Travis, not even a speck but I had to escape Sydney and Travis was the right cave.

"Sweet to hear; thanks Jay." His lips parted in a gentle smile. "So do you still preach at church?" I asked, trying to come up with a different conversation.

"I do but you distract me a lot, whenever I catch a glimpse of you I lose it, I mean I get them goose bumps." I laughed and he did the same. He was down to earth and I wondered why my mind was not totally equipped with him.

"Now you'll get punished by the heavens."

"I don't think so, the heavens know how heavenly you are and I'm pretty sure they want heavenly things for us, and I think there's nothing more heavenly than you in this world, heavenly character, heavenly voice, heavenly..."

"Stop it! You're going insane." I placed my index finger on his lips and he laughed, I needed so bad to love Travis, I wished to develop strong feelings for him but there were not any. There was a part of me that was glad for Sydney to be with Cheryl and me with Travis, maybe we were going to easily forget each other.

"Alright I'll stop but seriously, I'll be the happiest man alive to date a respectful virgin like you someday." I swallowed a lump that tried sticking on my throat and coughed a little while faking a giggle, a virgin title strangled me.

"I'm sorry to have mentioned it dear, just that I heard mom say it and I don't have any doubts about it."

"Yeah right!" I faked a smile.

"Now may I go please?" I tried freeing my hand from his but he squeezed me tighter. "I like you Jay, I mean it." He said with a serious face and I got confused looking at him.

"Jay!" My cousin roared behind me and I quickly released my hand from Travis's and shifted my eyes to him. He was advancing towards us slowly wearing the blue hospital gown and a blue trouser under the gown. His light complexion lightened up the whole corridor. Travis brushed my shoulders and left us standing there. Sydney's eyes were red with anger as he stared at me, disgust was written all over his face.

"Do you need anything?" I asked humbly.

"Just shut up and stop whoring around with morons while I die alone there." He howled and I trailed behind him silently while rolling my eyes.

CHAPTER FIVE

"Why do I get the feeling that you can't stand seeing me with Travis?" I asked Sydney as we reached his ward.

"Why the hell would I care? Are you my girlfriend maybe?," he said as he threw himself on top of the bed facing the ceiling.

"Sydney, just drop the pride," I grabbed a chair and sat beside him. "Whatever! I would be jealous if it wasn't him, he looks like he's sick or something g and I look way better than him," I rolled my eyes at his arrogance. "Yeah right. The last time I checked, that was called jealousy," I twisted my legs and mocked him.

"Suit yourself!" he added.

"Alright then good, and thank you for approving him for me, you're the best cousin ever lived," I giggled and he smirked.

"Yeah right? I was the worst cousin ever lived when I stirred up that cookie," he mocked.

"Ha ha ha, I no longer care keep mocking all you want!"

"So you like him that much?" he asked with a straight face, gawking at me.

"Why do you ask?"

He held my hand and drew me closer to the bed he was seated on. "Tell me truth, are you interested in that Travis guy? Don't you think you deserve more than just a mere nurse?" I shook my head and giggled for a minute.

"It don't really matter to me what he does, what matters is how I feel about him," I tortured him.

"Can I ask you something cuz, can we stay this cool until forever?"

"By this cool you mean listening to you talking about your boyfriends?"

I laughed a little harder.

"I enjoy it, we're back to being cousins and that gives me peace of mind, I can easily forgive myself and you."

"Well you're the one who couldn't stand my presence, I made you cringe but that won't stop the fact that I'm the virgin breaker"

"You now want to go there again really?" I stood up and stared at him in disbelief boasting around for destroying my world. "We'll never run away from this Jay, no matter how hard we try," he sat on the cold floor and leaned his back against the wall. His muscles popped up as he tied his hands around his folded knees, I sat in front of him and leaned my back on the bed and crossed my legs with his.

"I wish I were you, you sound like a person who lets go easily," I said with a sad face.

"Didn't you somewhat miss me? I mean through the hatred there must be a time when you thought the night was fabulous for us. It might sound horrible that your cousin took your virginity but it doesn't change the fact that I made you feel good," he laughed and I cringed sweetly as he lifted my chin and mocked me, I wanted so bad to hate him but I was slowly melting away and that sin was no longer eating away my conscience.

"Well it was beautiful yes, if you're talking about the romance and stuff, the sex was actually painful as hell," I never thought I would talk about the events of that night so openly but there I was.

"But you took it so well baby girl, it was the best day of my life," he said, and started rubbing my lips with his finger. "And I want it to happen again, and again."

"Keep on dreaming Sydney, that will never ever happen but dream on!" he grabbed my hand and sat me on the bed beside him.

"I don't mind dreaming, as long as you'll be sleeping next to me while I do it," he pulled me softly to his chest; and those wickedly beautiful feelings I had felt that night awakened. I breathed heavily and poked his irresistible muscles playfully; moving closer towards him, failing to ignore his physique and completely falling for him. He wrapped his arm around my shoulders and osculated my cheek.

"And as for what you asked, yes I get hurt when I see you with that nurse guy," he confessed at last. "You're supposed to be mine alone."

I nodded my head twice; convincing him he was the only guy I ever wanted. He smiled at my action and it felt good having his muscular arm around my body, them feelings that were long gone rained like manna back to me. He was one piece of magic, whenever he held me I lost all my powers.

"Are you okay?" he whispered in my ear, the hot air fueling my lust.

"Yeah, I'm fine. Just kiss me Sydney, kiss me and never stop. I can't pretend anymore," I swear I did not hear those words come out of my mouth but I said them. I knew it was the devil speaking not me. Our bodies connected leaving no space in between.

"And I won't leave you. I'll be here with you till you make it," I whispered, my feelings betraying me. I pressed tighter to him, wrapped my arms around his back and he ran his fingers through my hair and our foreheads came in total touch. I felt his cold lips on mine suddenly and I locked. We kissed. He sucked my lips like I was the last thing he was going to suck and I was reminded of the night I had spent with him, I wondered how after all that boiling hate I had for him I still missed him that bad. I felt his hands unfastening on my waist; I bind mine tighter to his head and suddenly felt his lips loosening too. I slowly pulled my lips out of the paradise unwillingly.

"Sydney, don't fear for me I'm alright," I whispered to his ear with my eyes still closed. As I tried dragging my lips back to the incredible moment, Sydney's heartbeat went beyond normal and his whole body went wet with sweat, his breathing rate escalated. I got the shock of my life and started sweating too. He lost his power and nearly fell and I caught him and laid him back on his bed. He lay in there groaning while fear gripped me by its abusive hand and I wondered what to do.

"*Cuz* are you alright?" deafening silence hit the room; only my loud exhaling could be heard.

With my pounding head I flew and called the doctor who came in as quickly as he could to check on him.

"What happened? What was he doing?" Doctor Dube asked. "We...He... He... was... running doc...I," I swallowed words and lumps, embarrassed again about my behavior.

"This person is still too weak to run Jay; I told you the rules didn't I?"

"I'm sorry doc, I just thought he has healed, just thought we could do some exercises. I was overjoyed, I'm sorry."

"No problem my dear, it's okay. He's going to be alright. I guess it's just the rise of temperature. Now go sit outside I'll check on him."

I did as I was told. I collided with Cheryl on the doorway. She was dressed to kill, a black ripped jean, red heels and a floral crop top. Her clothes showcased her curves in all their right places; she looked completely out-of-this-worldly. Her long weave was shining and neatly laid back, making her look exactly like an Indian since she was also light. She had a red lipstick and blue eye shadows and was carrying a blue clutch black and had bangles all over her arms. She looked so beautiful and I felt so embarrassed and a bit jealous because I was wearing a simple knee-length dress. If Sydney saw her like that, I was definitely going to be rejected.

"Jasmine!" she excitedly hugged me as I was busy examining her from head to toe.

"Cheryl," I said as we unplugged our arms from each other's bodies. I tried hard to make sure I sounded calm, since I was very scared of what I had just did with Sydney. It felt so unreal, after the years of dealing with guilt of my lost virginity I was throwing another bomb to myself.

"It's been long you know. I missed you a lot!" she grinned. "You are scarce at church and bible studies these days, that's the reason."

"Yeah, actually I was away at the rural area visiting my uncle. I came back as soon as Jenny told me Sydney wants to see me," she was blushing and I could see she had goose bumps in her tummy. The crush she had on Sydney was no child's play, she had had it long back when we were in high school.

"Alright I see. He's currently with the doctor so you can't get in right now. Maybe we can wait until the doctor leaves." "You're shaking Jay! Are you alright?" her smile faded and she moved closer and touched my shoulders.

"I'm fine, Sydney's temperature just fluctuated and I'm a bit scared," I looked down and shed a tear.

"Don't worry darling, I'm sure he's going to be fine. Just relax okay? You're a Godly woman, these diseases shouldn't scare you, just pray the fear off, and you always tell us that!" she rubbed my back and kissed my cheek.

"Thank you dear, thank you very much," I hugged her tighter and found a precious space to cry on, her scent was heavenly, like the one described by Solomon in the Bible's songs of Solomon when he praised his bride. I wondered how Cheryl could be so perfect.

"I'll get in and see him now darling, I'm failing to wait!" she blushed as she walked towards the door and marched in. I hurried to the waiting room and threw myself hard on the bench hating on myself for repeating the same mistake that had bruised me. When I saw Travis approaching, I pretended to be dead asleep. My mind was already burdened by a very heavy load, I needed not another load.

"Hey, woke up sleeping beauty," Travis shook me softly.

"You just dozed off on the bench; I can offer you a perfect place to sleep. Is everything alright?" he sat next to me.

"Hey Trav, I'm fine, just tired. I've been up all night," I failed to make eye contact with him; I thought his eyes would diffuse through my skin and locate my mind and my thoughts.

"Why? Did your cousin give you a hard time?" he threw me a worried look.

"No, he was fine. I was just scared you know."

"But you are kind of scared and your eyes are teary?"

"I said I'm okay Travis! I'm fine! Jeez!" I burst out with anger and he just stared at me pitifully, I looked down a bit embarrassed about my lashing out.

"Jay you can talk to me about anything, I'll always be here for you. Talk to me about anything, be it pain, joy and tears. I'll love everything about you, your mistakes I'll tolerate because I want to know you. I just need you to be open and free with me about anything. Please! If it's something bad happening here at the hospital or someone mistreating you." I sat up straight and stared at him wondering why he was not giving up on me.

"My mistakes you'll tolerate?" the words just escaped my mouth. 'What type of a guy Travis is? Will he tolerate me sleeping with my cousin? Will he tolerate me kissing with him on his sickbed? Will he tolerate my wolfish behavior adorned with a sheep skin? No he will never! I should never and I will never tell him.' I thought.

"I love you Jasmine. I mean it," the words were uttered with a heavy weight, with neither lust nor intentions. I stared at him, wondering where he got such peculiar behavior, Sydney would say those words while kissing my lips or holding my waist, but him, he sat a meter away from me but still said them with his eyes supporting his statement. I searched for a place in my heart, I could not find it. There was a block, Sydney.

"Trav, we'll talk. I've got to go," I stood up and turned to leave. Travis followed me behind and I bumped to the doctor whose face was written rage.

"How is he? Is he alright?" I asked curiously. Travis stood behind me and waited for the answer too.

"He is alright but there's a case I want to report to the police. These nurses are immoral. It seems like he engaged in some sexual activity, he needs not to be aroused at this moment until he heals, he's still weak for that, the rising of the temperature might lead to his death. This habit is growing in this hospital, nurses taking advantage of sick handsome men without their approval," he said with a heavy tone.

Brutal lightning struck across my heart and terror took over my mind. I endeavor with all my interior to never let any sign show through to Travis and Doctor Dube but my hands were shaking at the thought of jail. What would the church say?
How were they going to picture me? I was messing up endlessly without a halt.

"So, Doc any...any suspect yet?" Travis glued his eyes on me and I faked a smile at him and he faked it back.

"I do have a suspect but I don't know when she came over here," his hand rested on his chin and my heart failed to pump blood. What if he meant me?

"Ooh?" mouth wide open I mumbled.

"Yes, that unmannered girl who met up with you on the doorway. Did you see how disgusting she was dressed? I asked her to leave right away. I'll report this to the police," I took a deep breath and held my chest cooling down; I was not the number one suspect. Mr. Dube left us and Travis remained with me, he came closer and held my hand.

"Are you alright? Do you know something? I ask why you are shaking?"

"What? No Trav, I just, I need to see him..." he gripped my hand as I tried turning to leave.

"You are shaking a lot. What is your scared of Jay? Do you want to talk?" I raised my eyes and stared up at him. His eyes were full of love and passion.

"There's nothing to talk about. Sydney and Cheryl are going to be lovebirds soon, maybe they kissed, I know it's her and I'm just scared for her, she's my best friends. If that's all friends go please."

"Alright! But the doctor mentioned that you met up with her on the doorway, how could she? I mean when would she have kissed him?" he asked curiously.

"Travis what are you trying to tell me then? What are you saying? Tell me? Am I the one who aroused my own cousin? Are you trying to…."

"No no no! Jay c'mon I would never think so evil and low of you baby! I just felt like you probably know who did it and you are covering for them because of your Christian values and all," he said sincerely and I exhaled loudly, I was the one who was slowly selling myself.

"I don't know Trav, I saw my cousin shaking and got the shock of my life, I thought he was dying. That's the reason why I'm panicking," I said calmly.

"It's alright you can go see him," he let go of my hand and I hurried to the Sydney.

I reached the door and slowly opened it, Cheryl was sitting beside him, her hands tied around his body and Sydney stared at her too, his hand was also moving all over her, his other hand resting over her shoulders. I looked down with my embarrassment and jealousy reaching its culminating point, I cleared my throat to get their attention and they turned and looked at me. Cheryl was smiling endlessly and I read the news from that. How could Sydney do that to me?

"I heard your blood pressure had increased. How are you doing now?" I sat in the chair, far off from them. He gazed at me as if he was examining me from my head to my toes. His eyes were my second weakness; one glance from his eyes melted my problems like ice on the heat and he knew it.

"It wasn't so bad. I just got carried away and forgot my sickness," I looked away as Cheryl's eyes widened with shock.

"Got carried away with what babe? So it's true that all this is because of some sexual activity you had with someone?" she asked. I was surprised at her calling him 'babe' so soon, but it annoyed me.

"Me and Jay... we were... running, I forgot I was sick you, know, and thought I had completely healed, so I actually mean I got carried away running thing," he said and I despised every piece of him for scaring the hell out of me.

"Okay well then, because I took the blame, I was insulted by that doctor for being here . He thought I was the reason for all this! I love you Sydney and I need you so bad, but I'll never act sexual with you on your sickbed. I'll wait at least until you get out because me and you have a lifetime journey to take."

"He told me he warned you to stay away from him until he heals," I endeavored to halt the topic which was irritating my nervous system.

"Well, he did. I just needed to hear Sydney tell me he loves me and I've heard it you know. Tonight will be my best night; I'll sleep soundly because one of my cherished dreams has been fulfilled."

"I'm happy for you bestie! You have what every girl dreams of!" I faked a smile and Sydney looked at me and winked an eye smirking.

"I'll do whatever it takes to own this man, I know I haven't been a perfect and ideal girl but I'm leaving all my behaviors behind for Sydney. He's all I'll ever need," she said, tearfully staring at him as he blushed wickedly.

"Just one day dear and he's all you need?" I laughed mockingly, I could not take it anymore, it surprised me why she was all in after talking to a man for a few minutes and he was worshiping him in his presence.

"One touch from his hand was enough to show me he's nothing like all guys I've dated before. He's the one I want to call my husband in the future and I know I'll have to fight tooth and nail for me to own him because girls out there babe," I rolled my eyes and smirked.

"Yeah right. It's getting a bit late now darling he needs some rest. You'll see him soon, I'm pretty sure he'll be discharged soon. He'll then be yours night and day," I stood up, grabbed Cheryl's bag and waited on the doorway as she kissed his lips and his forehead. I waited impatiently; it was nothing funny for me. She came at last, all smiles and glows.

"Jay, thank you very much for doing this for me dear. You're indeed a true best friend. I don't even know how I'll thank you. I'll need billions of mouths to do that," she hugged me tightly.

"What are you even thanking me for dear?"

"Jenny told me you're the one who planned this, hooking me up with Sydney. The only man I've wanted is mine now Jay and all because of you! Thank you my friend," she hugged me even tighter and I took a long breathe annoyed.

"We're friends and you know and that's what friends are for, favors and all," I said as I pulled away from that uncomfortable hug and kissed her cheek.

"Bye now dear. Be well," I handed over her bag to her. "Thank you Jay, once again," she expressed her gratitude with her eyes and I faked a smile and turned to leave. I banged the door with so much power and leaned on it with my eyes closed and shaking my head.

"It doesn't feel good right?" Sydney stood up and headed towards me.

"What are you on about now?" I rolled my eyes and pretended to be off guard.

"The same feeling you have about me and this girl is the same feeling I have about you and that stupid nurse of yours."

"What are you even talking about Sydney?"

"I saw your every action when Cheryl was here, you felt like slapping her, you felt uncomfortable. You're not happy with this matchmaking you decided yourself," he laughed.

"You're imagining things, I'm cool with Cheryl, and she's my best friend for God's sake. She's pretty and she deserves you."

"I wish I had a best friend too, I'll be screwing his girlfriend, who'll be my cousin. Too funny huh?" he laughed so loud that his claws came visible.

"Stop it! Just shut up!" I turned and put my index finger on his mouth and he rubbed it off harder, dead in laughter.

"Let me enjoy my moment baby! I'm with you right now and it couldn't feel so beautiful," he said in between the laughter.

"We should stop this Sydney. I don't want to hurt Cheryl," the words came out of my deepest core.

"It's too late now sweetheart, these feelings we have for each other are far stronger for us to turn back now. I don't like this chick she's too forward," he was just being Sydney, always taking serious matters lightly.

"*Cuz*, I hate these emotional roller coasters I keep having., one minute I'm happy with you, the next I'm guilty and the next I'm scared. And I won't stop being scared now that the doctor said it's wrong to engage in sexual activities with you while you're sick. He told me they will find out who did this to you. What if they do Syd? I will go to jail. Its immorality, I'm a Christian, what will the church say?" I remembered my Christianity and died on the inside, God was watching me committing all those crimes and I did not even consider how He felt and looked at me.

"We should apologize to God," I said and he laughed.

"Jay, by sleeping together we've created a bond that we won't easily destroy and we're already connected. We'll never ignore that, so relax. It's me and you till time stands still, and besides, the suspected person is that Cheryl girl of yours because she cast smiles at me at the doctor's presence and he threw her out. So you're safe and sound, I won't let anything bad happen to you Jasmine, I'll protect you. I've had feelings for you since we were young and I won't let that go away," he sounded so relaxed.

"Are you sure that our secret is safe?" I held his hand and gazed straight into his eyes, searching for assurance in them.

"As safe as a skeleton in a closet," he stared back at me with a twisted lip in a very wicked smile. "What the hell is that supposed to mean?" "Come on Jay! Skeletons are safe in their closets ,aren't they? Maybe your mom got skeletons and you know nothing about them right?" The laughter proceeded until he lost balance and I just cursed him with my eyes and twitched my mouth, ,

"Sydney I beg of you my cousin, don't monkey around serious matters. This is the matter of life and death. Stop making fun of me and be serious."

"You know what I hate the most is that you don't trust me. Why do you panic when you're with me and I'm here assuring you that we are safe? That's a sign that you don't trust me and the choice I'm only left with is making fun of you Jasmine! Relax! I could say that in capital letters if I could! We're safe and sound and we're happy. I will never let any harm befall you," he said matter-of-factly and I smiled endlessly falling into his arms.

"You could've said this long back and I would have trusted you then," a gentle smile lightened up his face before he planted a gentle kiss on my cheek and tucked his head over my shoulders, and exhaled a bit louder, exhaling love, awakening my sleeping beauty.

CHAPTER SIX

The following morning was blossoming, it never blossoms when you are in a hospital of course because of the mourns of pain, of death, of turmoil, but the thought of my cousin making it again on the affairs of life made the day beautiful. I watched him sitting near the window, holding a window frame and staring with love at all the beautiful creatures that had fun outside in the warm weather. I went to and rested my hand on his shoulder and smiled.

"You're soon going to be a part of that," I said, massaging his shoulder gently.

"I never thought I'd live again. I thought my life was over and done with," he paused and shed a tear.

"It's alright; you've been granted another chance in life, forget the past and receive this gift," I had never seen him that emotional, it was tormenting me.

"Jay, there's God and I should've let you go offer yourself to him that night, really," he cleared his throat and swallowed a lump, with a look of worry across his youthful face. I felt my hand shaking on his shoulder and my face went red, I forcefully pulled it from that place it had gone to comfort and I faced the opposite direction from his. It was shocking to hear Sydney speak of God, it was not typical of him, it was scary.

"Where's this coming from all of a sudden?"

"You've always wanted me to be a Christian and now that I want to reward that to you you're going back to your stupid habit of halting important topics before they even begin," he howled angrily, stood up and grabbed my hand with force that instilled a pain on my poor little hand.

"I'm not disapproving you of being a Christian Sydney. I'm only disapproving you of opening oy healed wounds. Why are you sour all of a sudden? You're so unpredictable!" I said.

"A healed wound never opens again Jasmine!" he said. "Only a scar is left. If a wound re-opens, it was never healed at the first place, that's a white blood cell performing its damn function!" I saw some hot smoke coming out of his nose where his tear crossed. He swallowed some saliva and held my scared hand, I wondered where the solemnity was coming from all of a sudden.

"We kissed nine hours ago Jasmine and you told me it felt good but now that you're telling me about opening your wounds I know that you were just bluffing. The truth is, you're still hurting even after these two years and Jasmine I don't want to be a reason for your pains anymore. I've finally noticed there's God who saved my life after battling for it these weeks. As a result, this affair must stop; I'm giving you a chance to go back to your God. Focus on your Travis and I focus on Cheryl. Let's cut off these ties before one of us gets hurt," tears flooded on my dress and his were also flooding on his t-shirts. Maybe it was God communicating with me to stop my shenanigans and I had to obey.

"But yesterday you told me you loved me and you'll always be there for me. You assured me that our secret is safe and us too, you said you love me," I cried.

"Our secret is indeed safe Jay and we're safe, the only thing that's supposed to stop is this affair. I've come to my senses now, I'm sure you want this too. We can try it, let's please do this," he begged.

"Alright, Sydney I'm willing to try if that's what you want."

"Thank you Jay," we shared a warm hug. It was pretty different and it was heart-warming but deep down I was burning in pain, I had developed very strong feelings for Sydney and it felt so bad for him to 'break up' with me.

"You pack and I'll meet with mom and aunt outside right?" he patted my shoulders as he wiped his tears off and exit the door. I did not know what to do but I felt like I was freed from my lustful passions and I was freed from guilt at last. I went to the doctor and got all the medications and prescriptions for Sydney and then finished my packing. I sat up on the bed and stared into space, all smiles thinking of going back home, to church, to Bible study and prayer groups, it was going to be fairytale bliss, I hummed one of my beautiful church hymns.

"I'll miss you a lot princess, I was so used to seeing you every day," a gentle voice interrupted my beautiful thoughts and I froze like ice for minutes and came back to life after minutes after spotting Travis standing on the door with his hands on his pockets, his head leaning against the wall staring at me with a pretty sad face.

"It felt so good having you around, seeing you every morning distracted my mind from replaying scenes of dead bodies and hearing weeping voices. It didn't feel like a hospital at all."

"If you want me to come back and make your bitter days sweet don't you ever sneak up on me like that again," I giggled.

"I swear I won't do that again," his lips parted in a gentle smile.

"So, how long have you been standing there?"

"Long enough to know you have a nightingale voice that awoken all sleeping magnificence within me," I softened as I caught his eyes caressing me freezing on that warm snow. "I'm used to you preaching Trav when you speak like this... It feels, different," I sucked my lower lip and grinned. He marched in and sat beside me, took my hand on his, and intertwined our fingers. He was romantic, knowing how to show pristine affection, and I never sensed any lust in it, just truth. He earned a piece of me that day.

"I know right. I also never thought I was going to sit with a girl and find the right words to say to her. I've always been this guy who believes in a soul mate. Like I don't want to mess with a woman's body if I don't love her, I'll have that one woman who'll be mine for the rest of my life and maybe that's when I'll find the right words. When I met you Jay, and every time I see you, I just run out of words to say you know, I just feel idiotic, but I'm glad that I always say something right enough to be gifted this beautiful smile of yours," he said and I felt goose bumps taking over the throne inside my tummy.

"I...I...Trav, I too feel dumb right now?" I looked down and felt my mouth drying because of the shyness on my face and the ruling butterflies inside of me. He unplugged his right hand on mine and used it to lift my chin slowly bringing my eyes and his to the same position and they locked. My chest rose and fall at the way his eyes manifested his love for me. They were tender, passionate, and amiable and soft; they were soothing and life-giving. I felt like I had lost my memory and gazing at him was bringing back slowly. His strong arms tied my little soft body and he covered me in an affectionate embrace. It felt warm, and I clung so tightly like a baby would to its mother, I came to a realization that Sydney was right, we had to part ways and Travis was the man for me, I closed my eyes and got lost in that sweetest embrace, the one that dad, mom, aunt, Jenny or Sydney had never given me before.

"Jasmine, just don't ever forget that I love you," he said as he unlocked that hug.

"I promise I won't."

"Pinky swear?" he offered me his last little finger waiting for me to make a promise. I nodded and joined my little finger with his, sealing the promise. I then stood up and started packing the bags.

"Please give me one last hug before you leave," I laughed, shook, my head and placed my bags down and hugged him tightly again.

"I'm glad I'll see you at church now that this whole thing is over."

"I'll be there; I can't miss your sermons Pastor Travis," he laughed.

"Jay, what's taking you so long?" I wrestled out of Travis arms and nearly fell on the bed when I caught mom standing on the doorway. "Oh! Mom! I was just on my way out I..."

"It's okay baby," she looked at me smiling. Travis bit her lower lip in embarrassment.

"I'm sorry ma'am for keeping her this long. I shouldn't have," he said apologetically.

"No, it's fine my son. It really is. Help her with the bags," she smiled and I stared at her in total confusion of why she was not scolding me. She went out and left us trailing behind her, Travis carrying our bags.

"That was a close one huh?" he laughed.

"Well, I'm just surprised; she has never seen me with a guy before. I thought she was going to slap me but she's out here smiling like never before. It's weird."

"It's no secret that your mom loves me. I'm a well-mannered guy remember?" he said proudly.

"Don't celebrate yet, the night is still young," I laughed as we approached them, standing at the hospital gate. Aunt also beamed as she greeted Travis and took the bags from him.

"Pastor, we're honored to see you," aunt said as she offered for a handshake.

"Honored to see you too ma'am. However I'm not a pastor yet; I'm just a preacher for now," he giggled.

"I don't know how to separate the two, I always see you on the pulpit that's why," we all laughed aunt's joke, except Sydney.

"He's a great young man." Doctor Dube smiled as he pat his shoulders. Mom would not stop smiling at me.

"I know the woman who suits him the best, I wish I could do match-making right now," the doctor continued and I looked down and Travis smiled.

Aunt laughed and winked an eye at me, it felt so awkward.

"Are we going to leave or what?" Sydney said in irritation.

"We're going to leave yes baby," mom responded.

"I offer my peace to leave with you guys. God has saved your son's life. It makes me feel beautiful being able to save him from that tragic state. I also thank this cute young lady here who sacrificed her sweet home for her cousin's wellbeing. She took very good care of him and it was wonderful having her around. You surely know how to raise children ma'am, God blessed your womb," Doctor Dube poured his heart out and I cleared my throat and faked a smile.

"Wow! thank you very much doc I trust her on that one," Travis would not stop admiring me with his eyes.

"I cannot thank you enough doctor, words aren't enough to express my gratitude to you, when we first came here we had no hope of his survival," aunt said wiping tears with a tissue.

"Don't worry madam; God has not called him yet. I also forgot to tell you that something horrible happened. Someone tried acting wild on him and it was not good for his recovery, I'm still deciding on whether to open a case against them or not, I want an investigation to be done. I saw a young lady get in there dressed like a real prostitute, I suspect her," the doctor proceeded with the story and told them everything that he thought had happened to Sydney and my heart started sinking in fear. "What? Who?" aunt screamed angrily.

"Who could do that to a sick person for heaven's sake?" I trembled inside and wished to walk out of that scenario. Aunt was going mad and burning with fury. I tried so hard to not betray myself.

"And Jay where were you when it happened?" she caught me unaware.

"I...I had gone to...to the bathroom aunt," I lied and was sure my lips were shaking. Sydney cast an eye at me that told me to be brave or else I would betray us. "Disgusting you know," mom broke her silence.

"Girls these days aren't ashamed of themselves," I went red with embarrassment deep down.

"And you Sydney how could you let them? Go ahead and open a case doctor, this person must be arrested as soon as possible! We just can't risk, they did it to my son they'll do it to these other patients too," aunt howled and Sydney just rolled his eyes.

"Thank God my son's alive. If he were dead I was going to eat this person alive I swear."

The doctor was about to dial a certain number when I shouted.

"No doc! Don't," I ran and took his phone away from him and everybody gawked at me in confusion, Sydney's eyes told me that deep within him, he thought I was confessing.

"What? What's wrong my dear? Do you know who did this?" the doctor asked.

"No don't call the police doctor! It's a small issue and I'm sure Sydney is a grown-up guy, he knew what he was doing and besides, we're Christians, we are always taught about forgiveness. It won't look good for us when somebody gets arrested because of us. Let it go. The punishment will come from God," I spoke with determination, aiming for their belief in me.

"We cannot care about our reputation; this person is the one who'll have a tarnished reputation not us. What if she comes back and does the same to the other patients? Let's teach this whore a lesson that'll scare off other manipulators too!" she was breathing heavily displaying her complete disgust for whoever the person was.

"Aunt, actually it's...It was my friend Cheryl, so I'm sure we can do justice to her..."

"I've told you a million times to stay away from that girl Jasmine but you always protect her like you're her wings! Stay the hell away from her for heaven sake she's toxic for you!" mom screamed in agitation.

"I'm sorry mom. I really am, I didn't know she was capable of doing all this. She..." my tongue got stuck in between my mouth.

"I'll talk to her! I swear with my dead parents I'll strangle that horrible creature with my bare hands. Call the police doctor, what are you even waiting for? She deserves jail."

"Calm down aunt please. Don't you worry, I've already spoke to her and she apologized, she really feels bad for this and I'm sure she'll never repeat such a thing again," I swallowed too much saliva and that left my mouth dry.

"Why do you keep defending her Jasmine? You planned this together didn't you?" aunt shouted in anger marching towards me.

"Stop it mom! Why are y'all acting like I'm a toddler or something? Cheryl is my girlfriend and she was kissing me because I asked her to, I don't even see an issue in all this! I see y'all standing here discussing about me as if I'm not here, stop it, you're embarrassing me!" Sydney waltzed into the conversation and calmed the storm but boiled worst waves on aunt's head.

"Tell me you're joking because Cheryl being your girlfriend happens over my dead body! Never ever, not in this lifetime or in the life to come will you date that home wrecker, that moron, that..." she bit her lips so hard, trying to find the worst word that could fit her description of Cheryl as she was known for her unruly manners by everybody in the area.

"Calm down ma'am please. I'm sure this matter is already solved. Jasmine says this girl has admitted to her sins and asks for forgiveness. A guilty conscience needs no accuser they say. If Sydney says he loves her..."

"Would you mind staying away from matters that don't concern you please?" Sydney cut off Travis in a disheartening way and we all frowned so badly at him. I wondered what God he had experienced if he still had guts to piss off people like that. Travis maintained his silence and took a deep breath as he stared at me and I tried smiling at him.

"You know it's really hard to understand what's really going on here. This is real drama and to cut it short, may everyone leave in peace. What we wanted was our son to heal and now that he's fine I'm sure we have nothing else but gratitude. Let's drop this whole matter and leave it for God to deal with," Doctor Dube said and dismissed us.

"Very true. God will take care of this one, I swear," aunt said as she picked the bags and left before us, mom followed her too.

"Don't you ever, ever again jump into my matters; your opinion wasn't asked for anyway since this matter doesn't concern you," Sydney pointed his finger at Travis signaling a serious warning which scared and also enraged me.

"Sydney!" I shouted.

"I was only trying to shield you from your raging mom, I didn't mean any harm bro, but I'm sorry though if I anyhow hurt you," Travis lifted his hands in surrender showing his displeasure in squabbles.

"Fine! I'll appreciate it if you stayed in your lane bro," he said wickedly, dragged his legs and turned to leave. I took a deep breath as I stared at Travis who was confused too.

"What's going on Jay? Why is he overreacting to almost everything I do and say? He doesn't like me."

"Well, he sees you have a thing for me and you know how our brothers are like. They want to keep us toddlers and under their armpits till death forgetting we're growing up. You'll get used to him don't worry," I faked a laughter as he scooped me in his arms and hugged me tight.

"Alright, I understand now. I'll definitely be a good brother-in-law to him," he laughed.

"Don't get too excited, you haven't been rewarded that privilege yet," I joined him in laughter as he kissed my forehead and I turned to leave.

"But I no longer have any frights now. I'm convinced I'm a step away to my cherished dream," he waved and I nodded as I ran off to catch Sydney who was standing by the roadside hitchhiking with one hand inside his pocket. The taxi stopped just as I reached him and we got in and drove off. Janet had prepared breakfast for us as we arrived home. Aunt and mom were still complaining about the girl who had gone all sexual with my cousin and Janet caught the news. I had tried staying away from them and went to our bedroom clearing things up for Sydney and avoiding them but Janet still followed me there.

"Sis, who's that girl? Any idea?" what I had run away from had followed me to my hiding cave.

"No. They've already told you I was in the bathroom," I avoided her eyes as I spread the cover beds over the bed.

"Okay sis. That one is something else. Maybe she forced herself on him. Sex on the hospital bed?" what was she saying? Rumors had a bad habit of spreading and a lot of lies added along the way.

"No. It was not sex. It was only a kiss," I roared.

"How do you know? Maybe she did it, Sydney won't say,"

"I heard the doctor say it was a kiss not sex," I tried being calm and avoided her eyes every time she tried looking straight into mine.

"Yeah but whatever it was, it shouldn't have happened on a sickbed. Sydney should have said no too but hey I guess boys will always be boys," she said and helped me spread the blankets and I kept quiet, preventing the conversation from spoiling my mind. "And you're quiet Jay what's wrong with you? I'm sure you have a lot to say to me. I'm a whore and all but would never arouse a sick person; this girl has guts for days. Were you with Travis when this happened?" annoying questions ever and words were like a sharpest razor that cut me in two pieces. I wished I could share with Janet that I was the one who aroused my cousin's feelings but she had already judged that anonymous girl and would kill me if I confessed to her.   "I was in the bathroom Jenny. I know nothing about this," I was scared to reveal Cheryl's name because Jenny and Cheryl were too close, I knew she would have ran off and questioned her and I was going to be displayed for my lies so I stuck with my 'I don't know' answer.

"Alright I got that. I heard mom from a distance talking about Cheryl's name, it seems like she did something bad. Was it her? I sent her to come over there. Did Sydney see her? Are they in love?" Janet would not stop annoying me.

"Jenny! For heaven's sake I'm tired I need to rest. Why don't you ask Cheryl all these questions of yours through the phone?" I threw myself on bed in agitation.

"Fine!" she threw her hands in the air. "Forget about her, she'll come over anyway for Sydney. I'll talk to her. Tell me about you and the pastor are you guys dating?"

"Expect that, it's bound to happen" I assured her, changing my mood all of a sudden. She jumped up and down like a puppy, nodded her head smiling.

"Praise the Lord!" she shouted and I laughed as I stood up from bed.

"I'm happy for you sis. At least you'll be happy now. Travis is a good guy you know. And you'll be meeting up with him at these prayer bands and Bible study groups of yours. I'm sure mom will be happy to hear the news. She hungers for a good guy for you. He is the one perfect match for you," her words assured me.

Travis was liked by our church members a lot. He was good at preaching and singing too. He had a Degree in Medical Science and was furthering his education to a Masters Degree and training to be a medical doctor. Travis came from a well respected family and his parents were educated and well known for guidance and counselling. His father was a lecturer and a pastor, his mother was a Headmistress. Therefore my plan of dating Travis really fired my imagination. It was going to cover my dirty little secret with my cousin and would relieve my mother.

We all spent the afternoon sleeping and when evening approached, Aunt prepared supper for us as we were all relieved to have Sydney out of his grave and back home. She was a good cook and her meals were tasty and delicious, whenever she cooked everybody would feel an empty tummy.

"Unfortunately, tomorrow we're going back guys," aunt said with a look of worry as we sat for supper.

"I have to go back to work and Sydney needs time and space to heal. He will come back when he gains back his life," that felt like a stab on my heart. I did not know why but I still needed Sydney to stay with us a bit longer. The first thought told me being away from Sydney would make me forget about him, and the other forced me to fight hard for him, he had to stay.

"Come on Aunt! why so early? At least let our cousin stay back with us. Please aunt," I pleaded with her, reminding her with my eyes of how beloved I was to her.

"No honey, he's still weak as you can see and you guys have a lot to do. Nobody will be able to take care of him, he will come back after recovery I promise and I don't want Janet's friends here arousing his feelings. I don't want any girl from this place to hook up with my son, unless that girl has your manners. That Cheryl is a beast," her face said it that she was never prepared to leave Sydney with us. So aunt wanted a girl like me for Sydney? Why the hell was I made to be his cousin?

"But I'm there Aunt, mom will be working and Janet is going to school the day after tomorrow and I'll be all alone. I'll be lonely, I need something to do. At least let me take care of him. And besides, I'm the one who was given the prescriptions by the doctor; I will look after him Aunt. You said you will be at work and nobody will take care of him at home. I don't want anything bad to happen to him, I've come too far to let him go with you now," everyone was speechless in the room, I know they were surprised, I was the same girl that had hated Sydney with perfect hatred. Sydney was smiling and staring at me in admiration.

"Alright, alright then Jay, he's all yours, what can I say?" aunt threw her hands in the air with surrender.

"Sydney, seems like you'll remain behind with your beloved cousin." "Thank you mom," Sydney said licking his lower lip and winking an eye at me.

"What are you thanking me for? You mean you never wanted to go too?" aunt opened her mouth in amazement. Sydney laughed.

"I need to return favors to Jay, she gave me life remember. It would hurt leaving without repaying what she did to me and besides, we just reconciled."

"This is one unbelievable act! Jasmine and Sydney are fighting for each other like hell after the hell they've been through with each other. God works in mysterious ways," Janet clapped as she stood up and headed towards our bedroom.

"I need to start packing," aunt said.

"We like it this way, this is what we call a family, happy family," mom cheered. I needed to ask for a cell phone from mom so I could chat up with Travis but I was scared because I had believed she had suspected something about me at the hospital when I begged to remain with Sydney. I stood up and headed to our bedroom where I prepared a room for him. I and Janet we're going to sleep at the living room. Aunt shared a room and a bed with mom.

"Jenny I have Travis's number with me here, may I please use your phone chatting with him," I blushed as Jenny cooled with enthusiasm and handed her cell phone over to me. I saved his contact and went away from Jenny to chat him up on WhatsApp. He was online.

Me: Hi it's Jasmine. (Pause and long breath).

Travis: Oh God! I've been waiting for you to text all day long. I miss your face. (A smile on my face)

Me: That's my little sister's number you may use it for now if you wanna chat me up. Him: Do you love me Jay?

Me: (Close my eyes and blush and Jay laughs) I think I do but may we please meet if you get time.

Him: I can't believe it's you who's asking to meet up and I can't say how much relieved I am to hear from you Jay.

Me: I'm not that scarce Trav.

Him: Don't be late then I'll wait for you.

Me: Where?

Him: I'll call you dear.

Me: Alright then goodnight.

Him: Sleep tight beautiful.

I breathed as I handed the phone back to Jenny who jumped at me laughing loudly. I laughed along with her, my plan was going to succeed but I felt bad for asking a boy to meet up with me. It was better than kissing my cousin though, so I had to do it. I was going to ask mom to buy me a cell phone the following day. I slept soundly on the couch with my little sister next to me holding unto me so tightly it felt so good to have her by my side.

CHAPTER SEVEN

Janet was the first one to get up and go shopping for her boarding groceries as she was going to leave for school the following day. I woke up after her and started tidying up and heating water for mom and aunt who were going to leave early; mom for work and aunt returning back to Cape Town. I prepared breakfast for them, hot coffee and toasted bread. I also had breakfast early because that was the day for my date with Travis.

"Mom I think it's the right time for me to own a cell phone now," I said as I joined them on the table after serving them breakfast.

"What happened now baby? Why do you need a phone?"

"Nothing happened mom, I think I'm old enough and I'm also tired of Jenny bragging about hers to me," I blushed, covering my face with my hands. "Okay baby, your phone was bought yesterday, seems like it's a coincidence that you thought of your phone while I was doing the same. It's on the wardrobe, on my grey handbag. Use it wisely."

"Thank you very much," I was so relieved so I left my food and ran to her bedroom, unlocked the wardrobe and took my phone out, inserted the sim card and put it on charger smiling endlessly. Mom and aunt laughed at the way I was overjoyed by owning a phone.

"I'm leaving my niece; won't you wish me well?" aunt shouted as she opened her arms welcoming me in.

"I won't sleep a wink if I won't wish you a God-guided journey aunty," I said, laughing and progressing towards her and wrapping my arms around her with love. "I'm going to miss you a lot," I said in between hitched breaths.

"Don't worry Jay; you will be with me soon. Just focus on finding me an educated husband who'll take this virginity from you," she laughed and turned to leave. If only she knew that her wicked son had done that already.

"Don't worry aunty, I'll get you one."

"And don't ever forget to keep that whore away from my son!" she warned.

"All sorted aunty, I've got this."

He and mom also bid Sydney farewell and left. I turned towards the bathroom to freshen up for my date with Travis. I had to look gorgeous so as to let my beauty blind his love.

Janet had not returned yet and Sydney was still in bed. I opened the door slowly and he was awake staring at his phone. He shifted his attention towards me as I entered the room. He was topless and it took my breath away eyeing all that and a bag of cheese. "Sorry to disturb you Cuz, I'm here for my clothes and creams," I said progressing towards the wardrobe.

"Where to?" he threw his phone on the bed, stretched his body and sat up straight, brushing his muscles aggressively.

"I have a date with Travis," he raised his head slowly and glanced at me, shook his head and took a long breath.

"Where is my breakfast?" he stood up slowly. He did not seem to be in pain anymore.

"Kitchen."

"Thanks for letting me stay by the way," he said and progressed towards me.

"It's alright, thanks for allowing me to date Travis freely too, and for also agreeing to be nothing else but my cousin."

"Really?"

I stood lifeless like an idol in front of the wardrobe as he came and lodged an inch in front of me. He could have covered himself with blankets until I left the room but he chose to flaunt with his boxers just to abuse my soul. I tried so hard to take my eyes away from that tempting sight and I kept rubbing my head now and again. As I raised them up, I saw his manhood full inside his black underwear. His masculine iron-made thighs flowed with greenish youthful veins and his legs hairy.

"You keep trying to convince yourself that you want that idiot when in reality you know you want me. You won't resist me Jay; you'll never, not even in your wildest dreams. This Travis thing just sucks and whatever I said in the hospital was because I was overjoyed about leaving the hospital," his lips curved in a devilish smile as he lifted my chin with his middle finger. Lust filled my nostrils and I lost my breath when my eyes stole a stare at his face, his hair neatly cut, and beards well shaved. There was a line that connected the hair and the side beards, and its dark color lightened up his face, his wolfish eyes mocking me and his lips, well set, full and parted.

I felt my mouth watery and I glued at him with my heartbeat zinging and my lips parted as I drew a startled breath and in that instant, he pulled me closer and touched my uncovered shoulders with his masculine, as warm a winter blanket and he left it wrapped around me when he brushed his lips on mine adorably. I pressed onto him tightly and he bent his head on me and my lips parted and I closed my eyes as I felt his cold lips dipping slowly on mine. He mesmerized my lips so softly like they were some delicate object and I was drowning in that heaven when suddenly a voice broke forth on the door which I noticed was not even closed.

"Jay, where are you?" I quickly pulled myself from Sydney with a huge force and I fell hard in front of the wardrobe. I used that opportunity to kneel and pretend I was searching for my shoes on the lower shelf of the wardrobe. Sydney laughed and grabbed his bathing towel and covered his lower part of the body as Jenny hurried into the room. "Jay, I've been calling you for hours. What are you doing here?"

"I'm looking for my shoes and I'm here to change for Travis. You know, the date," I did not look at her, in case my face betrayed me.

"I see, why didn't you let Sydney out, he's half naked, his muscles are a temptation, you don't want to end up in trouble," she giggled jokingly. Did she also have feelings for Sydney?

"They must be tempting to every girl but not me, I'm different," I said. "And you? Are you done with your shopping?" I stood up. Sydney laughed again and bit his lower lip as he applied toothpaste on his toothbrush. I cursed him quietly as I fought hard to change the topic with Jenny. "No, that's why I'm here. I need Sydney to go and help me carry the groceries. He needs to meet up with Cheryl, mom and aunt are boiling about her so I guess she cannot come here," she stared at him and I did the same.

"Oh, talk to him. I'm not sure if he can carry heavy objects yet though," I licked my lower lip wishing he would not agree. I did not want him out of the house, not with Cheryl.

"I will go with you Jenny. I'm fine now and Jay knows it," I frowned, he knew how to piss me off, he also knew how to turn me on.

"What does he mean?" asked Jenny.

"Sydney is Sydney, then y'all wonder why sometimes I hate him. Anyway I'm on my way to Travis now," I curved my lips in a smile, Jenny smiled too.

"I need to freshen you up Jay, you look terrible," she sat me on the bed and applied her creams and powders on my face. She chose a little red half-dress for me and applied a red lipstick on my lips, I had been a girl who loved natural more than artificial but to be noticed I thought I had to apply makeup like every girl so Travis would have never thought I was dumb. She chose golden heels and gave me her clutch bag and a sandy watch. My natural hair was neatly tied at the end as it was long and ebony.

"He won't resist you sis trust me," Jenny admired. "Damn girl!" we noticed Sydney standing on the doorway staring straight at me with his big soulful eyes full of jealousy. "You've even changed yourself for that slut?" he added. "Sydney stop being rude! That guy is every girl's dream. I once had a crush too," Jenny defended.

"You're crushing on every guy on this planet Janet, you're just a whore like your sister," he rolled past me to the wardrobe and pulled his jeans out, wore them and a white skinny t-shirt. "What? I'm not a whore! What do you mean I'm a whore Sydney?" I defended myself, noticing Sydney was trying to destroy my world in a flash just because of his jealousy.

"Oh! Yeah, you're not a whore, you're a sweetheart. You're good at everything from kisses to...I mean everything."

"As if you've ever tasted her lips," Jenny rolled her eyes. I frowned so vicious at Sydney and he laughed at me mockingly. He was trying to make me feel bad so I could cancel my date with Travis.

"Anyway guys, mom bought me an expensive phone. Give me your numbers!" I smiled, flaunting about my new phone. "Now adultery will be a lot easier huh?" Sydney called again, abusing my emotions was his goal so I would not go out with Travis.

"What adultery now?" Jenny asked as we all walked out of the house and me saving their numbers on my phone.

"I mean Travis and hers... yeah, I mean them, their love sorry, not adultery actually," he chuckled and Janet joined him ignorant of everything that was going on. I left them laughing and marched off toward the shops.

As I approached the restaurant, Travis was there sitting on one of the white chairs wearing a black suit, looking fine. I progressed towards him as he stood up and offered me a warm hug. "You're late Jay, I have been waiting," he kissed my forehead. "I'm sorry Trav, I was doing something," I remembered that I had received another kiss from Sydney and it was all I thought about, it was stuck on my mind like a tattoo.

"How are you anyway?" I took a seat opposite of him.

"You look stunning Jay, but I don't like makeup that much. And please don't get me wrong, I just mean, you're beautiful the way you are and if you did this to impress me baby just know I prefer the real you, I so much love your natural beauty," I looked down embarrassed a bit. Sydney had admired me and there was he thinking I had overdone myself.

"Well, I'm sorry too. It's my little sister who insisted it on me and I did not want to disappoint her," I lied.

"There's no problem Jay. How's your cousin doing?"

"He's fine, let's not talk about him," I faked a smile. His name got me smiling, thinking about everything we were doing together behind closed doors.

"You're so angelic when you smile like this," he held my hands and stared admirably at me, I wished he could know who was the reason behind that smile.

"Thank you Trav. Anyway, I've decided about me and you, we do have a chance."

"Oh! just like that?" his eyes widened.

"Why the hesitation? I've made you wait for too long and I don't see any reason why I can make you wait any longer. The moment we had yesterday at the hospital must've proved to you that I really am fond of you too," I smiled and took his hand on mine. He smiled back at me curiously.

"Wow, this is like music to my ears you know. I can't believe I've won your heart so easily Jay, I mean it's unlike you, you were too hard, I thought you were gonna make me chew stone's for another week," he glowed.

"I know. Get used to it then. I'm yours now," I blushed.
"I'm already starting to get used to it. You're a nice woman Jasmine,"   "I'm flattered thank you," I giggled a little.

"What to order?"

"Don't worry, I don't have much time. Mom will skin me alive if she finds me outdoors, I really have to go back," I stood up and picked my clutch bag from the table. I was not enjoying the moment with Travis, it felt so boring, all I wanted was Sydney, he was all I could think about. I merely wanted my family to believe that I was dating Travis, he was my cover up, I loved Sydney.

"Come on! you've been here for only a few minutes and your mother knocks off by dusk. Please Jay, stay with me for some time," he stood up, pulled my hand to sit me down and I pulled back.

"I'm sorry Trav, but you know my cousin is still unwell so I'll have to make sure he's well taken care of. We'll talk over the phone. I wanted to let you know that I love you and I wanted to say it to you face to front but I'm not here to stay."

"What cousin are you even talking about Jasmine? Isn't he the one I saw with his girlfriend just a few minutes ago before I pulled over here," my eyes widened. "Oh! His girlfriend?" I said in embarrassment.

"Your friend Cheryl of course and they were all cozy," he looked at me with a puzzled face.

"Jay what's up?"

"Nothing Trav, you know the incident that took at the hospital. He still needs not to be aroused. I'll have to take care of him, aunt gave me that responsibility, you had how much she hate that girl and I don't have a choice but to do as she says. Please allow me to go," I begged, faking it because deep down I wanted to run off and leave his presence with or without his consent.

"No problem, please give me a hug," I reluctantly hugged him and he kissed my forehead and I waved and left.

Millions of thoughts were pondering on my mind as I ran by and there was nobody at home by the time I reached there. I dialed Sydney's number and dropped it before it rang. I wanted him to be home with me not to roam around with other girls. Jealousy had struck me hard; I could not imagine any girl with Sydney getting what he had given me, that breath taking kiss. I dialed a few times still dropping and the last one went through. I shook with fear, I wanted to make him jealous when I went out with Travis but jealousy hit the wrong person.

"Missing me already?" his voice was full of mockery and wickedness. I cursed him for that.

"Where are you? You need to have your lunch and medication," I said, making sure my voice was not betraying my emotions.

He laughed diabolically.

"I'm on my way, I missed you too," I dropped the phone and blamed myself once again for respecting my wicked feelings. I knew he could read through me when everybody was failing to. The door swung open as I was busy beating myself up sitting on the couch. Janet and Sydney walked in carrying the groceries.

"Sis Jay, you're back so early? I bet you didn't even kiss the poor guy," Janet laughed at me and I kept quiet and stared angrily at her. "I understand sis, your first kiss has to be special and with the person you love the most."

"Shut up Jenny." Guilt struck me badly.

"Fine sis Jay, you're a Christian and I believe your first kiss will be after marriage in Dubai during your honeymoon," she laughed mockingly and Sydney stared at me and shook his head laughing.

"I heard you were seen with Cheryl?" I directed the question to Sydney angrily.

"We're lovebirds and that one you know and that one you organized," he winked his eye with a reason to hurt me and turned to leave. I shook with terror. Janet looked at me and I faked a smile at her.

"But you heard what Aunty said Sydney! He advised me to keep you away from Cheryl. You should've stayed home!" I burst out unreasonably and Jenny's eyes widened.

"And don't tell me you're going to do that sis Jay? Adults will always be adults shouting at us for everything. You'll never keep your best friend away from Sydney right? Because that will break her heart. She loves him completely and Sydney saw it today. And we planned this together and we're going to protect these two!"

"That's true, the feeling is mutual. Cheryl's a wonderful girl and is willing to give up her bad behavior for me, what more could a guy want. I got what I wanted and you too, I'm pretty sure you and nurse have hooked up."

"Your lunch is on the microwave Jenny. You'll dish up for your cousin too. I need to sleep," I said calmly as I went and locked myself on mom's bedroom and cried myself to sleep. I was feeling so complicated, not knowing whether to be happy or sad. Sydney was playing mind games with me. He had done the same too on the hospital and he was never giving up with hurting my feelings and causing me emotional roller coasters. He and Cheryl were never going to survive on my watch I swore.

"Baby, what's wrong? Your eyes are red, you've been crying," mom wake me up.

"No mom, I'm fine. I'm sure it's because I've been sleeping," I lay on her lap hiding my face.

"There's a WhatsApp message on your screen," I peeped on my phone and there was a text from Travis. 'Missing you already.' I knew mom had seen it, hiding it would be stupid. I ignored it, closed my eyes and breathed heavily expecting a very hard slap from mom. I went back to her lap and heard another notification tone sound. I raised my head and on the screen was another Travis' message 'Honey, are you there?' I grabbed the phone and hid it under my head quickly. I raised my eyes slowly to look at mom and I caught her staring at me smiling with love and joy. She was smiling at me and nodding her head. I was embarrassed but I smiled from the inside, mom liked Travis and she thought I had a right match on him. She hugged me tightly and I smiled enthusiastically, knowing my plan had worked.

Mom was relaxed and she was okay with me.   "I'll pray for you guys," that's all she said as she went out of the room leaving me rolling on the bed with some nasty happiness. I followed her to the kitchen with a glowing face. Everything was alright, I had thought. Mom went and bought takeaways for all of us and urged us to cook not, I knew she was celebrating my love story with Travis. She even sang a song for us and everybody was surprised to see her on that level of happiness

CHAPTER EIGHT

"Sis Jay! I have a great idea and I'm sue you'll like this one!" Janet hopped with enthusiasm and I grinned curiously, we were spreading our blankets on the couches at night when mom was in her room, Sydney was sleeping too.

"Let's hear it ma'am. What is it?" I said.

"Sydney has invited your friend Cheryl for a sleepover tonight and I'll go out for a sleepover at my boyfriend's. How about we invite your new boyfriend over here too," she whispered in my ear so that mom could not catch a word of what she was saying.

"Are you being serious right now?" I asked, eyes wide open, she sat down on the sofa rolling her eyes.

"Alright then forget about Travis, it was just an idea for God's sake. Cheryl and I will do what we're good at, while you stay boring like always. I just ask you to safeguard us from mom and aunt," she rolled her eyes and threw her hands up rudely.

"Sydney is still weak Jenny and you know arousing his feelings can be dangerous in this condition. Please leave him alone until he's okay!" I pleaded.

"But Jay you were all smiles last week about this relationship. You're the one who even made Sydney stay and not leave with aunt, why these stupid reasons all of a sudden?" she roared.

"We need to keep low profile Jenny please, you know very well how our parents feel about Cheryl," I begged her. "That's

116

exactly what I'm trying to do here sister but you're pulling in a different direction."

"Janet now I'll have to remind you that Sydney is under my care. I'm the one who was told the do's and don'ts by the doctor. I do not have a problem with him and Cheryl, all I want is for him to completely heal before committing all the wild acts he can. It's still too early for all that. They shouted at me when his temperature rose at the hospital that day, I won't allow such threats to run on me anymore!" I fired back.

"I'm sorry sis Jay, but I'll have to disrespect you just for today. We've already made these plans and we won't cancel them because of you," she said as she picked up her phone and ranged Cheryl who could not resist but came in like five minutes after the call. She looked all beautiful and curvy in it and insecurity hit me hard. I cast a nasty look at her as she arrived but she smiled at me instead.

"Jay, I missed you, my friend. You aren't coming to church these days and there's no sign of you at the Bible study groups," she hugged me and I stood like a statue responding to neither her words nor her hug.

"So you're here for a sleepover with a sick man? huh?" I teased.

"The last time I checked, we were taught not to sleep around at church, or maybe I attend a different church from yours?" I added.

"And the last time I checked, you weren't this acidic, you were soft. The last time I checked, the last time you attended church was two weeks ago, meaning you're no longer a part of us right?" she clapped back and heart slammed.

"I'm still the same person and I love my friend so much to let her rot in sin. And for your own information, the reason why I'm not attending church these days is because I'm taking care of my sick cousin," she smiled, flattered by my words which had that exact motive of flattering her.

"I know you like me a lot Jay but don't worry. I'll be alright, I'm used to this. Sydney loves me a lot and I love him, I promise to be a sweet sister-in-law to you," I faked a smile and she laughed thinking I was convinced when in reality I was burning with fury. I shook my head and went to the couch and let them discuss their plans which I swore to destroy and confuse.

"It's fine my friend, please don't hurt him. Be gentle with him."

"Now this is Jay I know," Jenny whispered sweetly playing with my cheeks in excitement. "We need to wait for mom to fall asleep and I'll escort you to him," she said.

"Goodnight and goo luck guys," I threw myself on the couch and covered myself with the blankets.

After mom could not be heard humming, Janet and Cheryl sneaked into our bedroom as stealthily as cats. I felt my heart beating faster inside the blankets that I failed to even breathe. Wrath burned within my veins and beads of sweat ran down my face as I remembered Sydney's kisses and his touches, all that was going to be Cheryl's for the night! I swore to fight and I threw the blankets in the air and rushed to the bedroom where I stopped and peeped through the door and I saw Cheryl seated next to Sydney, massaging his shoulders in a sweet way that planted a grimace upon my forehead. Janet was changing her clothes as she too was going to leave for her boyfriend's place.

"You look beautiful baby," Sydney complimented Cheryl after he spotted me peeping on the door and I knew his words were aimed at making me hurting me and making me jealous and he prevailed on that one.

"Thank you baby," Cheryl blushed and kissed Sydney's cheek. I went back to the sofa sweating and I grabbed my phone and dialed my mother's number. She answered in seconds.

"Hello Jay, are you okay? Aren't you at home why are you calling me?" she asked and I wished she could calm down and not raise her voice so they would not hear her.

"I'm fine mom, just woke up and go to our room and see for yourself what nonsense is going on. I'm dropping this call now," I exhaled loudly after dropping the call and dipped myself into my blankets pretending to be asleep and waiting to hear the noises after mom would spot them.

I heard her storm inside the room roaring like a hurricane.

"What the hell is going on under my roof? Janet! Do you want to send me some early grave?" I heard mom shouting and judging by the silence in the room, everyone was freezing to death.

"I'm sorry aunt, I really am," I heard Sydney say.

"Sorry for what Sydney? Didn't Maggie warn you enough about this girl? Do you even care about your health?"

"Mom for heaven' sake can't we make our own decisions and choices without being judged and insulted everyday? I won't tolerate being treated like a toddler anymore, I'm a grown up girl. Sydney is a man and he's allowed to also make his own choices" I heard Jenny disrespecting my mother like that and I fumed with anger, wishing I could give her a hard slap but I had to pretend to be dead asleep to save myself.

"Go ahead and disrespect me Janet, I know you're a curse anyway, your disrespect doesn't surprise me no more. All I want is this whore out of my house now!" mom boiled and I smiled from the inside.

"I'm really sorry aunt, I really am. I'm no longer a whore I promise, I love Sydney with all my heart glad he's from this family. I've changed my ways; please allow me to stay aunt please," I heard Cheryl beg and I understood she was really changing; she was never the type of a girl to she had been exactly like Janet but the way she begged made me realize she really wanted to love Sydney.

"Oh my God! She says she's not a whore when she goes around kissing sick people at the hospital, that's a definition of a real whore baby..."

"What? No! I didn't do that! I swear, I'm not the one who kissed Sydney, he can confirm that aunt! Please ask him," I wished to hang myself on that very moment, I was being exposed, why would I called mom at the first place?

"I don't have time for games and I'm not your aunt, we know the truth and we won't monkey around it right? Now take your ass and leave from here now!" "Aunt please..." she begged.

"I said get out!" I heard sounds of footsteps and I knew she was being pushed out of the room, she and Jenny approached the sitting room and I opened one eye and peeped at them, Cheryl crying and Jenny disgusted and my heart melting at the beautiful scene before me. Jenny shook me up and I woke up, rubbing my eyes like I had been sleeping.

"What's wrong Jenny! You just disturbed my beautiful dream," I faked a deep breath.

"Good for you, you're busy having beautiful dreams while your mom is chasing us out of her house," she rolled her mouth. "What? How did she come to know? I'm sure you guys spoke louder. You'll have me killed; I'm a dead person walking now Jenny do you see what I was talking about? Mom will tell me aunt about this and she'll skin me alive. Oh ,God!" I left the couch with my hands on my head and roamed around the house shedding crocodile tears.

"Relax Jay; I'll cover for you okay? Relax. I'll handle mom and aunt. Just be calm," she came and hugged me.

"I'm one shattered person now! I feel like I'll never love Sydney freely, there are always blocks and I don't know what to do." Cheryl said tearfully and I went and knelt beside her and wiped off her tears.

"Relax my friend. The matter I spoke about is still a block for now but they'll be fine as time moves on. Maybe you and Sydney need to meet in a different space. This home is just somewhere you cannot bubble in, you know the rules her. Just relax; Sydney is all yours, me and Jenny will see to that. If God wants you guys to be together there'll be no blocks," I offered her fake assurance from deep within.

"It's true Cheryl; we'll definitely let Sydney love you without blocks we promise," Jenny assured.

"What am I without you guys? Thank you very much and I promise you I have changed completely, I want to settle down, please help me convince your parents on that one," we all smiled, nodded our heads and unplugged the hug.

"Sis Jay, let me escort Cheryl back home. I'll be back in a few minutes okay? I'm no longer interested in being with my boyfriend I'm pissed off," Jenny said as she picked Cheryl's clutch bag and marched towards the door.

"Wait Jenny! Cheryl needs love and company right now in this state. Won't you just go and spend the night with her? I'll cover for you," Cheryl smiled like she had just won a trophy; she could not believe my kindness.

"Why didn't I think of that first? That's an awesome idea sis. I'll go and spend the night at her place," Jenny said as she nodded her head and awarded me a smile too.

"Jay my best friend you're an angel you know that! Thank you for everything you're doing for me dearest," she said in-between happy sobs.

"The bible says a friend loves all the times darling you're my best friend and it's my duty to take care of you."

"And believe me dear, I'm the most blessed girl on the planet to have you as my friend," she waved as they closed the door and left. I took a deep breath, game well played.

I was craving so bad to be around Sydney, I went and showered with cold water and I felt a bit better. I went straight to our bedroom and opened the door slowly. The lights were on and he was lying on top of the bed still shirtless and staring into space, I had wrapped myself in my bathing towel. I sneaked in and slowly headed towards the wardrobe. I applied my body cream to my body; I needed to wear my underpants hence he was supposed to face the opposite direction for a few minutes even though I needed so bad for him to catch a glimpse of my unclad body, I found a chance to speak to him.

"*Cuz*, may you please excuse me for seconds I need to dress up," he shifted his attention towards me and I dropped the towel a little lower leaving half of my breasts visible so he could notice me, my conscience was not with me.

"Since when do you bath and dress up so late at night Jasmine?" he asked as he turned to stare back at the wall. I felt bad that he did not have any compliments on what he saw.

"Dress up, I'm staring at the wall," I wanted him to notice my beauty. With my towel still wrapped around half of my body, I went and sat on the bed facing the opposite direction.

"*Cuz*, we need to talk," I spoke slowly.

"I knew it you miss me. You are full of drama you know that right?" he turned back to look at me.

"What drama are you talking about Sydney?"

"I know you're the one who informed aunt about Cheryl being here," he stared straight into my eyes and I got a little uncomfortable.

"Don't start with your accusations, I was asleep," I pointed a finger at him. "And you don't start with your lies Jasmine. I saw you remember? And I knew that you were not going to have a good night."

"I didn't do anything," I looked down embarrassed but feeling incredible that Sydney knew it but still kept it to himself.

"We both know you're lying. I'm irresistible, whoever I touch won't go away from me, but I was trying to do you a favor since you're my cousin. I thought this would be a good opportunity for us to stay away from each other. You was with the Godly man, doesn't he touch you like I touch you?" he placed his hand on his chin staring at me. I looked down and rolled my eyes. He shook his head and breathed.

"I'm failing Sydney; I'm failing to forget about that day, about the kisses. I think about it every second and you're all over my mind. I'm trying but I have this huge love for you and I can't ignore it, I've prayed and it won't go away. You won't blame me Sydney; you took away my virginity for heaven's sake and these days all I think about is you," he stretched his hand unto me and I held onto it and he pulled me closer to him, we sat facing each other on the bed.

"You don't know how healing and beautiful those words are, especially coming from you," he blushed and I blushed back, covering my eyes with my hands shying away from his wolfish eyes. "I just wanted to hear you say it baby, I was just kidding that we should stay away from each other."

"One day I'll die because of you," I said softly.

"I'm sorry baby," he took up both my cheeks with both of his hands and it could not feel so lovelier.

"It feels nice getting lost with you. Where I am right now is where I want to be forever," he breathed and laid his head on top of mine with surrender and love.

"I'll do whatever makes you happy," I smiled and he laughed.

"But you know you're so dramatic, you were sweating with jealousy. You missed me right?" I slapped his cheek in a loving manner. I was feeling whole and complete with him. I felt safe and sound with him. Everything made sense when I was with him and I was assured he was the love of my life. He was all I needed.

"Sydney, nobody will ever make me feel as good as you make me feel. I love being here with you," he was playing with my cheeks in a lovely manner and I shivered at the way his eyes fondled me. He licked his lips and kissed my cheek.

"Don't even say that, I wish you weren't my cousin. I wish there was no culture thing. I would do everything with you. My wishes and my goals on you," he placed his hand around my waist and pulled me closer to him while I stroked his beard. He playfully bit my finger with his teeth and I giggled. We gazed into each other's eyes for long.

"I love you Jay," he whispered into my ears, sucking my earlobe sending shivers of desire to my skin.

"I love you even more Sydney," I took a long breath.

"And your goals and your wishes on me, I wouldn't mind if you fulfil them, as long as you'll stay with me like this forever," I poured my heart and my soul unto him.

"Let's come up with a solution today sweetheart, I love you and you love me and we're in love. We're making it official today; we have to stop these emotional games we play with each other. Let's just pretend to love those two people in the face of the world but keep our thing strong," he said.

"Good idea, please don't make me jealous anymore."

"I promise I won't."

Travis never made me feel the way I felt when I was with Sydney and I swore Sydney was the one for me and I kept on telling myself it was God's will to make me find love under the roof. He was playing with me, rocking with me, showing love to me. I had found somebody for me and I believed God had sent him.

"It's windy and cold outside can you feel the breeze?" his eyes lightened up and his manly smile tickled my inner core. "I feel the wind and I feel you baby," he slowly lowered his head and reached for my face.

"Jay, remember we were about to kiss when Janet walked in on us earlier, you left me thirsty for you. What do you have for me today?" he reached for my lips, his chest rising and falling, fueling my lust.

"Everything Sydney, my body, my heart, and my soul," I clung unto him viciously as our lips met.

"And I have everything you need honey."

The night was dirty.

CHAPTER NINE

The morning was a bit freezing and I was so reluctant to get out of bed but I had to do it quickly so mom would not notice I did not spend my night on the couch. However, the way Sydney's hands were wrapped around me was so heavenly and irresistible so I stayed a little longer and watched him sleeping soundly. I was surprised and relieved that regret was no longer there; my love for my sweetheart of a cousin was growing. Whatever I had done with him last night felt so right and it was nothing like the heavy, life-threatening guilt I had felt during the day of my ordination at church. I kissed his cheek softly and glowed as I slowly got out of bed, it was Saturday, the day of the Lord when I was supposed to be worshipping and connecting with the supernatural spirits. I hummed church songs as I heated water for mom who had to go to church. My sudden lost of interest for church was suspicious, all I wanted was to remain back home with my Sydney.

"Let's go to church baby, we'll be late," mom advanced towards me completely dressed and ready to leave.

"Mom, I was just heating water for you and I even made breakfast!"

"What? How could you even switch on the stove knowing every well it's Sabbath? You cooked? What have you done Jay? You know very well that we don't cook on Saturdays? Wait? What happened to you? Are you my Jasmine or the other?" mom cried out, if there was one strict rule in our family, it was the Sabbath rule! We were never allowed to touch anything on the Sabbath. "Oh! I'm sorry mom; I don't know what's on my mind really?
How could I forget this?" I said, realizing that my love for Sydney was really getting in the way of everything including my faith.

"This is the mistake I don't expect, especially from you Jay. You've never committed this one before, not even one day. Is it love on the brains?" mom asked, jokingly but solemn at the same time. I knew mom meant Travis. I blushed, I was only thinking about Sydney. "Anyway let's leave, we're getting late,"
"Oh mom, I won't go today. I'm not feeling well," It was my

third absence at church and the whole week I had not gone for Bible study. I had stayed indoors to 'take care' of Sydney.

"Again you won't go?" she asked, puzzled. "What's wrong?"

"It's nothing serious mom, I guess it's the sleeping posture on the couch you know, and my whole body just aches," I faked a giggle.

"You've spent many days without church baby, it's never a good thing for you and today Travis will be preaching," she smiled and winked an eye. I pretended to blush so mom could think the mention of Travis's name melted my limbs.

"You may go with my phone mom, so you may record the sermon for me. I bet he's a real pastor," I handed her my phone which I knew had nothing fishy.

"I'll do exactly that beloved. You got yourself a good man, I'm no longer stressed about you, I knew that you would never disappoint me," she smiled, kissed my cheeks, and turned to leave.

"I love you to mom, pray for me," I waved as mom left.

I had woken up all glowing and happy but my mother's proud and determined words about me changed my mood all of a sudden. Tears stood on my face remembering how much of a heathen I had turned to be. The last thing I needed to hear about at that point was the bible. Every verse would remind me of how much of a sinner I was. I then turned to her bedroom and threw myself onto her bed. I could not believe I had done it again, worst part on a Friday night, the Sabbath had already started and I was supposed to be worshipping God in preparation of His Holy Sabbath. It felt so unreal to me so I forced myself into believing it was all a worst nightmare.

I sat on my mother's bed and folded a pillow in my arms, remembering how I had committed a very huge crime in her bed. A picture of mom and dad's wedding hung on the wall and I wondered how my dad would have reacted to everything I had done if he had heard it while he was alive. I closed my eyes trying to imagine how his face would be like after hearing the story; it scared me so much hence I opened my eyes. My dad had been my hero, making sure I had all I had, the best education and motivation. He had worked hard just to make sure I was safe and secure and I had promised him to take care of myself. Their wedding picture reminded me of the good old days when I had dreamed to wed. I had promised mom to keep my body pure until my perfect white wedding and my marriage, but I had broken the promise. As I knelt down to pray Sydney knocked on the door and came in uninvited; I quickly wiped away my tears so he could not notice that I was crying and quickly got up and sat on bed.

"You should not walk around like this, what if mom was here?" I complained as he was only wearing a black short trouser.

"I knew you were alone. I heard your mom leaving," he moved towards my mom's wardrobe. "I can't find the toothpaste on that shelf, that's why I came here." He knew how to walk like man and I blushed, knowing he was mine only and he loved only me.

"Last night was incredible, thank you for last night," he said as he applied the toothpaste to the toothbrush. I got embarrassed and looked away shyly as he flashed his masculine smile at me.

"Stop it Sydney, your breakfast is ready you may go and eat now," I turned back to face the headboard. I was cursing him but deep inside I wanted him to stay there with me, his voice opened all the locked doors inside of me.

"Do you want to know what I'm thinking about? Our first night on this bed, it's a memory to retain," his voice was dripping honeycomb. He moved closer to me, picked me up from the bed and held my waist. I was melting away, all the guilt went off with the rivers of joy that swept through me as I hung on those hands that felt like bronze on my skin, hurting me beautifully.

"It was one of the most beautiful yet hurtful moments of my life, I shouldn't have regretted babe," I spread my hands on my face blushing and he pressed me tighter. I was never trying to make him feel bad; I was giving him even more chances. "You loved it, that's what matters the most. It was true when I said it yesterday that I love you. You need not worry about who's going to say what. I'm with you in this and we'll explain to them that we love each other. Rituals will be performed to cleanse us. Don't be scared a bit, it's a common thing nowadays for cousins to marry. It'll be a very beautiful thing to our parents
I'm telling you," he laughed as he put me down and hugged me. I smiled thinking about rituals that cut all relations between the two families and allowed the relatives to get married, my dream was coming true, I was getting married to the man of my dreams.

It had been long since I had last prayed. I had stopped praying the day he stepped out of the hospital bed. I however still felt like God was forgiving me and giving me chances, I thought He was the one who delivered Sydney for me, if He never wanted me for him, why would He keep on giving us chances together? He wanted us to get married, I thought.

I put the sheets to the bathroom for washing and Sydney followed me there.

"How do you expect me to finish my washing if you keep on nagging me like this?" I joked with him and he pulled me back and I fell on his chest. We cuddled. When I was with him there was no place I could have rather been.

"Let them soak up. I need you with me here," he placed his hands on my chest and planted kisses on my forehead. The sitting room door blast open as we were busy caressing each other and I pushed him back, he managed to stand up and reach for his toothbrush and I stood rigid. It was Janet. She peeped on the bathroom and saw us, she advanced towards us. She gawked at us and I tried so hard to ignore her. I prayed she had not noticed anything.

"What's wrong with you two?" she had her hands on her waist and wore a confused face. Sydney proceeded pretending to brush his teeth and I tried so hard to make sure Janet's eyes did not see the sheets. Unfortunately they did.

"Jasmine my sister! I can't believe you're washing on a Sabbath! What in the world is wrong with you? Is your love for God fading? Why are you here? Why aren't you at church?!" she stared at me with a questioning look. I trembled and shook with fear but made sure I managed to cover my fears up. "What's wrong with you Jenny? What's with all these endless questions?" I roared at her my voice mixed with both confidence and fear. I glanced at the sheets and went red. I cooked up a lie.

"Sydney was vomiting all night and woke up to these dirty sheets, I have to wash them. And besides, the bible says its right to do well on Sabbath; do you want me to let my cousin sleep on stinking sheets because it's a Sabbath?" I confidently said.

"Sorry sis, it's just that mom pissed me off last night and I don't know how to deal with her. Cheryl loves Sydney, she's been crying all night begging me to find a way to convince mom that she's a changed person."

"Poor thing, she'll be fine," I said as I advanced towards the sheets and started washing them.

"And you cousin? Why didn't you even fight for her? You kept on apologizing endlessly."

"I respect my elders, I'm respectful," he said, brushing his teeth aggressively.

"Whatever guys, anyway I'm leaving for school today. I can't stay under this roof no more. I leave Cheryl under your care Jasmine, good thing you have a cell phone now. You'll communicate with her and inform her every time when mom is not around so she can come over," she said as if giving me rules and I would get a slap if I could not do it.

"Fine ma'am. It's all good," I said as we headed towards the room and I helped her pack her belongings and groceries. She dressed up and I wished she could leave earlier because she was disturbing my affair. I kept on looking at her, wishing she would not look at my cousin and had the same feelings for him like I did.

"I'm leaving sis, be well!"

"Bye," I said without any hesitation and she turned to look at me in disbelief.

"Just like that sis Jay? You know Jay you've changed a lot since you came from the hospital. I wonder if it's that Travis guy. Anyway bye sis. I hope you enjoy whatever is giving you so much joy these days. You no longer care about me, because the Jasmine I know would have given me a hug and some comforting words, quoted from scriptures and all. I don't understand this beast in front of me anymore," she turned to leave and my heart bled. Those words felt like a sharp stab in my soul. I had not noticed my change of behavior except the fact that I had stopped going to church and assured mom that I did pray and would remain back home to look after my cousin. I loved Sydney though and he had assured me that he would stand by me through thick and thin and that he loved me too.

"I'm not sure Syd, don't you maybe feel like the drum is about to burst? I feel like Janet suspects something," I said with a look of worry across my face.

"Don't worry about her. She's stressed up, she'll be fine, she's going to school anyway we gave all the house to ourselves," assured Sydney.

"Now come and help me with the dishes."

I followed him to the kitchen and helped him wash the dishes after getting done with the sheets. The door swung open and mom got in, catching us washing the dishes chatting and laughing together. She frowned at me. "Jasmine, I saw the sheets hanging on the washing line. Since when do you wash on Saturday? I'm tired of telling you this one thing I swear, you're being disrespectful and I can't take it no more!" mom roared once again about the same matter she had been shouting at me about in the morning.

"Sorry aunt, I've been throwing up and I messed the sheets up, I'm the one who asked her to wash them for me," Sydney came to my defense and I let out a long breath, he saved me. "Oh I'm sorry dear, are you fine now?" mom brushed his shoulders.

"I'm fine now aunt, I'm stronger," they laughed together and I stood up to serve mom her lunch.

"Travis preached baby. He is talented that guy," mom said as she sat down on the couch smiling and nodding her head.

"He spoke about being true to yourself, to God and to the people around you," the glass I was holding fell down and broke into pieces. Mom stood up and Sydney frowned at me. I was shaking at mom's topic, I had to avoid it. I felt like it was directed to me.

"Oh mom, sorry I broke your glass."

"Are you alright?" mom progressed towards me and helped me clean up the pieces. "You're not well Jay."

"No! I'm okay. The glass slipped through my hands mom." I stopped her.

"So Janet left?"

"Yes she left" I sat down after serving mom.

"Wow, just like that, anyway good riddance. My sweetheart of a child is still here with me," I had started hating hearing mom speaking of my perfection when Sydney was there. He knew I was not what people thought I was. I faked a smile and thanked her.

"And about that record, I will listen to it mom," I said getting up to wash the dishes but mom took them away and washed them up.

"Yes please do, you'll understand you fell in love with a pastor himself, and I can't wait for you to be a shepherdess" she laughed and Sydney frowned at me and mom caught him.

"And that unpleasant frown?" mom asked Sydney and he nearly jumped, he did not know that mom was watching him.

"Oh aunt, it's nothing, Jay didn't tell me she's in love," he defended himself.

"Oh she didn't? I'll share the news with you myself. She's not only in love but with the perfect man in the planet. I know and believe that her father will rest in perfect peace now that she has this perfect man for herself. Your cousin has really a good choice," mom was smiling with pride and I was making funny pauses in my face, biting my tongue, sucking my lips, taking heavy breaths. Sydney was still casting glances at me.

"Wow, that's great aunt, that's good," he faked another smile.

"Not so great, soon, he'll marry her. I told him to never touch her till marriage, and he promised me he has no evil intentions just love and respect for her. He promised to marry her soon despite her finishing her education, he also promised to find a varsity for her if I fail to."

"Oh! aunt ...I mean yeah, will you let him?" Sydney was red with jealousy.

"Without any hesitation or second thoughts! I trust that guy the way I trust my daughter. The neighbors know about it and everyone is just so happy and approving of their relationship."

"Alright aunt. Great."

"I'll prepare supper for you guys today," she said happily.

I stood up and went outside to clear my head, how could Travis talk of marriage? I thought as I went by. I took a small path that led to the bushes and a small stream, I needed to sit there and think but unfortunately I heard Sydney's footsteps behind me.

"I didn't think this Travis thing was going serious to marriage? I thought you loved me! When will you leave that chameleon?" he hissed as he trailed behind me.

"Sydney we spoke about this please. I don't love him, he's just a shield, he's the surface and you're the real meaning baby," I used an endearing tone so he could calm down and he did. The last thing I needed was drama when everything was going smooth in the eyes of everyone.

"I hate hearing his name under this roof over and over again and I guess you understand, your mom is all hyper and excited over him. Will he ever approve me?"

"Don't worry, when the time is right we'll let them know," he blushed.

"I'm thrilled by the fact that it's you and me now and we've got us to ourselves."

"But Sydney, don't you think we're giving clues everywhere?" I said as we approached the stream surrounded by thorny trees, nobody would be in that place. We sat down on some green grass just besides the stream.

"I no longer care about the clues; I just think this Travis is going too far with this! I won't let him marry you," he swore. "He'll just play you."

"I want to get married to you Sydney," I blushed.

"Just the way I want to marry you sweetheart, and I'll also fulfil your varsity dream you need to not worry," he gave me a long, warm hug. "I love you Jay."

"I love you too Sydney."

"Now let's go back ho..." something interrupted him and he stared everywhere but could not see anything. "What?" I asked a bit scared and unlocked my body from his. "I think I heard footprints," he said, his eyes still roaming around the place.

"Nobody visits this place frequently honey, might be falling branches or something," I assured him.

"You're right. Let's go babe, I need to watch some movie on YouTube now," he grabbed me by the hand and lifted me up. "You can go love, I'll stay behind I still need to enjoy seeing the trees and the sound of falling waters," I smiled as he grabbed my waist and brought me closer to him.

"As long as you'll be safe I'll be alright," he said as we kissed for a few minutes.

"Bye baby."

"Bye honey," I waved as he left and smiled.

I felt clear after Sydney told me that he too wanted to marry me, that he would finance my varsity. I loved Sydney with my whole heart and had become addicted to him in every way. I was definitely going to get married to him.

"The relationship you share is so strange you guys," I nearly popped up as I caught Travis standing beside me. I held my chest and breathed heavily in shock and fear and also burning curiosity of what exactly he had seen me doing with Sydney.

"How long have you been standing there Trav? Don't sneak on me like this you scared me," I stood up again and hugged him. He hugged me back but not as tight as he used to.

"Long enough to see your cousin kissing you, on your lips," I felt my heart breaking into a million pieces. I released myself from him and stood numb for like five minutes thinking of the words to say, I had to be strong. I had to protect myself from any mess. "What the hell are you even talking about Travis?" I faked anger while guilt was rising within me.

"I'm talking about what I saw Jay, how could you?" he stopped and looked straight into my eyes; and I had to make sure my eyes did not betray me too. "You need to get your eyes checked then my dear. And you need to not let your brain conclude on things it doesn't know," I hissed. "Sydney is still not hundred percent healed, I take walks with him to these kinds of places to help him stretch and stand properly, he kissed my forehead goodbye as he left since I told him I needed time alone to pray, and you're accusing of the worst thing ever. I can't believe what I'm hearing now Travis," I shed crocodile tears and put my hands on my face.

"Oh! I'm sorry then Jay. I thought he was kissing your lips, I was surprised really."

"But how could you even think of such a thing Travis?"

"Jay I'm sorry, I really am. Don't get me wrong please; I just thought he was kissing you. I'm sorry. I saw the posture you guys were in and concluded my story, I didn't want to believe it also, I'm sorry that my eyes deceived me," he took my hands from my face and apologized even with his countenance, I was glad to win again.

"It's okay, please don't accuse me of such things, you hurt me Trav," he wiped them away and kissed my cheek.

"I'm really sorry sweetheart, maybe I'm getting obsessed with you too much. It's just that sometimes I feel like you spend a lot of time with your cousin more than I, and that you love him more than I," he said as he sat me down on the grass and joined me.

"It's not like that babe, the love I have for my cousin is different from the one I have for you. He's family and you're my boyfriend. I was just helping him heal. God would punish me if I left my sick cousin uncared for just to be with my boyfriend. I hope you understand," I assured him.

"You're a nice person Jay, I know that and I believe you'll be nice till God rewards you for everything you deserve," he said and I got a little panic attack.

"Yeah Trav, anyway, what were you doing in this bush?" "I was praying, this was my fasting day so I had to move away from home, after preaching I had to just be out in the bushes," he was indeed serious about his relationship with God and I was thinking how broken mine was.

"So what were you praying about?" I asked, remembering how much I used to fast in my days of my purity.

"You won't believe it babe," he held my chin.

"I was presenting our relationship to God, telling Him I love you and He knows my love for you is true and pure. I prayed for Him to be the foundation, for Him to lead us and to give me the strength to face whatever might come up in future. I think you're my future wife Jay. I used to pray a lot for God to show me a perfect girlfriend and my feelings for you couldn't fade, I knew you're my answered prayer."

"Trav, it's getting dark, we need to go," I stood up; the weight that his words carried scared me to the core. Travis' love for me was different from Sydney's in every way. He was not hasty, not lusty nor jealous. It was something I had never known, something I was scared to know. He stood up too.

"No problem sweetie, I don't want your mom to slap you," he held my hands.

"Did she tell you she warned me about you?" he laughed. "Yeah, she did," I faked a smile, I wanted to be away from that scenario, Travis' truth scared the hell out of me.

"Yeah, I told her to relax. I have no evil intentions with you. I'll take one step at a time. It actually surprised me when I found out she knows about us, I wanted me and you to get to know each other well first before engaging our parents into this, but its cool honey. It's not like I don't know how your mom the way mom loves you, that she'll stalk every detail about your love life," he was something that nobody in the world could understand and I felt bad for having had spilled the beans to my mother about him when he had different views.

"Trav, bye baby," I tried releasing my hands from his but he held me tight and stared at me with love, true love and passion that terrified me. I gathered courage and raised my eyes and stared at him too. I saw him, the cornea, the irises, the pupils, his eyes. No lust, just compassion and love.

"I love you Jasmine. I love your imperfections, I love your heart, and I love your soul. I want to love you till the end." "I...I...I love you too Trav," he gently planted a long, warm kiss on my forehead. He did not care about my lips at all. I wished I had loved him first, with a smile on my face I pulled my hands from his and turned to leave. After a few meters I peeped through my shoulders and saw him still standing on the spot staring at me, I waved and he waved back.

I had to choose.

Time was ticking.

CHAPTER TEN

Weeks passed and I conquered a dilemma of who to choose between Travis and Sydney. I managed to leave my brains out of my affairs and only engaged my heart and as a result, my affair with Sydney grew even stronger that I even convinced myself I was going to get married to him for sure. I gave up on trying loving who my heart despised because Sydney showed me love every day even though we were trying with all our powers to keep our affair a secret still. We would walk together to the shops without people curious about anything. He even prompted me to start plaiting my hair and I did since he financed everything. I skillfully committed adultery under my parents' premises without thinking twice or regretting it. Travis did call me almost every day; and I would answer his calls privately and only when mom was around, what he was to me- a shield for covering my adultery. I wanted to keep him closer to me so mom would keep thinking I was his and our love was growing stronger.

Saturday found me numb because I had been working hard preparing for Sabbath that Friday.

"You are a million miles away baby, would you mind sharing what's on your mind?" mom revived me from my deep thoughts on the Saturday afternoon as we sat for lunch. I was leaning on a couch with my hand on my cheek and the other hand carrying a spoon, staring into space.

"Oh! mothing mom. I'm just feeling down today," I took my eyes from wherever they were focused at and stared back at my dish.

"It's because you didn't go to church again. I'm failing to answer millions of questions from the church members about your whereabouts; it's been five weeks now for heaven sake!" mom cried out.

"I know mom, I'll go next week I promise. Sydney is completely fine now and this coming week I'll go. He's been holding me up."

"Please do so! because next week I'll tell the pastor that our youth leader is now a fulltime heathen," mom smiled and I faked one too.

"I think I'm not feeling well mom, I'm feeling cold and nauseous since yesterday," I said as I folded myself on the couch.

"I saw it. Let's just hope its nothing serious baby," she said, pushing a spoonful of rice into her mouth.

"It might be because I worked very hard yesterday preparing for the Lord's Day. I carried very heavy objects and I'm pretty sure my body is now reacting to all the backbreaking jobs of yesterday," I said, yawning. Sydney was silent and busy helping himself into his food. He stared at me and shook his head.

"I'm sorry my baby you should get some sleep. I'll do the dishes."

"Yeah mom, I really should because I don't even have appetite for this rice," I stood up and headed towards the bedroom, feeling dizzy and my head heavier than before. Sydney followed me there.

"You're still failing to relax right?" he said as he closed the door behind him.

"I'm relaxed babe; I'm really not feeling well. I feel weak and sleepy," I rolled my head on his chest as he sat next to me.

"Meaning you're sick for real or you're just hovering over your fears of being caught," he laughed and I blushed a little.   "I know you. You're a softie, a scared little cat."

"You should've helped me with the work yesterday; I wouldn't be sick right now," tears formed in my eyes and he shook his head and went and picked two tablets from his bag and offered them to me.

"Drink this, they're pain blocks and I'm sure they'll block every pain in your body," I drank them up.

"Thank y......" I did not finish the words as I threw up all the food I had pushed inside my body including the tablets.

"Jay!" Sydney gazed at me with pitiful eyes.

"You're sick for real."

"Get me some water; I need to brush this awful smell off," I said as I headed towards the bathroom and he proceeded towards the kitchen. I was sure he told my mother I was throwing up and she hurried in like a whirlwind.

"I don't want to take chances with you Jay, let's go see the doctor now, it might be serious," she pulled my hand and we hurried to change clothes.

"I'll escort you guys," Sydney said as he also went to change. We were done within fifteen minutes and hired a taxi that dropped us at the hospital gate. We met up with Doctor Dube on one of the corridors that led to his surgery and he stopped us as he removed his glasses as he saw us approaching.

"Laurie! And your kids and my two favorite people in the world! I'm happy to see you! And I can see he is a John Cena now," he laughed as we exchanged greetings. The doctor knew mom from the clinic, which was the reason why he even knew her by name.

"We're all still strong, except for one of your two favorite people, she's not well as you can see her," mom said as we walked slowly towards the surgery. "What's wrong with her?" he said as he held my cheeks and played with the like I was a toddler. "You know her and her love for God. She has been working all day yesterday in preparation for Sabbath, watering the garden, plucking up weeds, doing the laundry for everyone, sweeping, cooking, everything doc! She just doesn't want the Sabbath to be tainted, now all the hard work has made her body to react," mom said laughing.

"You've got yourself a jewel here Laurie, you have fifteen cows already," he laughed as he stared lovingly at me.

"Say that again Doc," mom laughed again.

"But don't worry; I'm sure it's nothing serious. The two of you may sit outside I'll check on her," the doctor said to mom and Sydney who obeyed quietly and sat on the bench just outside the surgery as I followed him in. He pulled the chair and made me sit as he moved and sat on his behind his desk? He was a nice old man, approximately in his mid sixties; I was completely sure he chose being a doctor because that was his purpose in the world. "Where exactly does it hurt my daughter?" he asked, pulling a pen from his briefcase and writing on my book.

"I actually don't know where it hurts. I'm feeling very weak and dizzy, my whole body just feels complicated, and it's something I've never felt before. I can't eat, I've lost my appetite and I'm throwing up a lot," I said and he put his pen down and stopped writing and gazed at me.

"So it's nothing like a backache right? Maybe you ate something that just doesn't sit well with you. Ever been tested for HIV?" He asked and I opened my eyes wider.

"What? no! Could it be HIV? Is that what you mean?" I trembled with fear; I had never tested for HIV before.

"No daughter, don't get me wrong. I'm just asking. I'm wondering what your sickness could be. I trust you a lot; I know you're not the type of a girl that sleeps around. However, testing for HIV and knowing your status is essential, remember it's not only with sexual contact that you can get infected but through sharp objects too. You never know, we need to get you tested for that one," he said as he stood up and searched for something on his shelves.

What if Sydney had it? He was the only guy I ever slept with and my heart was banging at the thought of being infected with HIV. He progressed towards me with his kit.

"Alright stretch your hand," I stretched my hand and he put the thermometer under my armpit, testing my temperature.

"Your temperature is very high dear," I trembled. Further tests were done and my BP was high too.

"Now I'll test you for HIV my dear."

I exhaled in and out loudly, with fear overtaking my world. He planted an injection in my skin and it sucked blood out of me. He then gave me a tissue paper and I sat there in discomfort.

"If there are two lines on this test it means you're HIV positive, if there's one, you are negative," he said.

"Doctor may I go to the bathroom for a second please?" I asked in fear.

"It's alright, take this thing with you and pee on it the get it back to me," he said and offered me something that looked like a stick. I stood up and left, peed on that thing then gave it back to him.

Failing to hold myself, I went out and joined mom and Sydney outside the surgery, I was shaking with fear.

"What did he say baby? you look scared," mom asked and Sydney curiously gazed at me.

"He's testing me for HIV mom, I'm scared. What if I've got it?" I placed my hand on my mouth with tears falling from my face. Sydney rolled his eyes and shook his head.

"So you think I'm HIV positive right?" he lashed out at me and I nearly froze. "Wait!" mom hushed, looking puzzled just the same way as I was. How could he say that?

"What do you mean she thinks you're HIV positive?" the way he rolled his mouth showed me he recognized his blunder. "Oh aunt, I mean Jay is a virgin and there's no way she can have

HIV, I mean she spends her days with me and it's only my blood she has touched when I was sick. So that's why I'm thinking maybe she's scared of that one."

"Oh silly!" mom laughed, "you nearly scared me,"

"You just relax baby, the doctor just wants to test everything so he could be sure of what the problem is. There's no way you can be HIV positive," mom declared.

"I need the bathroom," I stood up again and ran towards the bathroom feeling very uncomfortable and the smell of pills and medicines in the surgery increased the level of my dizziness and nausea.

Sydney followed me there and found me throwing up once more.

"I'm scared Sydney," I said as I washed my face and wiped my mouth with water. I progressed towards Sydney who scooped me in his arms and kissed my forehead.

"I'm clean baby, there's no need to worry. They did tests on me when I was sick and I was negative, I'm pretty sure about that one. Please relax, it's just a normal sickness," he gave me a ray of hope and I faked a smile.

"Just go back and relax okay?" he rubbed my back and kissed my cheek as we returned back from the bathroom. He got into the surgery with me, and we did not find the doctor, he came back shortly after.

He entered slowly and leaned his back against the wall and stared at me without winking his eye. I lost the ray of hope that Sydney had planted on me and shock seizures got the better of me. We both stood up and cast glances at each other in despair. I breathed heavily. Where would I have gotten it if Sydney was clean? I thought as a silent tear rolled unwelcomed to my face. Sydney also looked puzzled and confused.

"Doctor, so I'm HIV positive?" I said as I stood up and held my head with both my hands.

"No, you're clean," he uttered unhurriedly.

"I told you so," Sydney burst out rejoicing. I held my chest with both my hands and thanked the heavens as the doctor handed me the results in that test, one line! I was surely clean. A clear, untainted smile radiated through my face as I stared at Sydney who also gazed back at me with a smile.

Mr. Dube still did not move but glued his eyes at me like a crocodile. They were mixed with pain and hurt. He looked so disappointed and I failed to read the whole story on his eyes. "Now what's wrong Doc? she's clean, what else is left that you want to tell us?" Sydney asked, wearing back the puzzled face. The doctor folded his arms on his chest and kept his silence still looking at me and rolling his mouth and shaking his head.

"Stop giving her that look, can't you see you're scaring the beast inside of us?" I saw the flesh in Sydney's forehead folding like a paper in a heated frown as he progressed towards him. Mr. Dube tried to push him and failed, but managed to pull himself out of his swearing hands. He was breathing heavily his eyes wide open in both fear and anger. We all stood still, Sydney burning in anger and me shaking in fear. Mr. Dube calmed down, wore his jacket well and came closer to me.

"My son, I'm still older than you and you don't need to react this way with me," he spoke calmly.

"I don't care! You're scaring us and we want to leave, you're talking your time and it's getting dark outside," Sydney spoke rudely and I gave him a bad eye.

"I'll apologize then for that one, I'm just so disappointed at your cousin. I need no fights now." 'What is he talking about?' I stood there being a victim of curiosity; he was disappointed in me why? I could see Sydney getting annoyed by that doctor who would not stop beating about the bush with serious matters. I did not answer him. "Well, I can see that your mouth is glued now."

"Will you stop that sh*t and tell us what the hell is going on?" Sydney was reaching his boiling point.

"Alright then, as you wish, so will it be. Your cousin is pregnant, your test came back with two lines."

A huge lump rested in my throat and I stood wide eyed like an owl wishing for tears that disappeared to heaven knows where. The thing I feared the most had happened to me, all that time I was having sex how could I forget about pregnancy? I watched the frown unfold in Sydney's face; I lost my power and threw myself hard on the chair and took my hands back to my head. I was pregnant and that too with my cousin's child. The doctor kept quiet too, still staring at me in disbelief. There was a deafening silence at the surgery as everybody had their thoughts pondering on their heads, some with disbelief, some with guilt and regret and some with fear and pain. I laid my head on the table and all thoughts ran away from me, I felt empty. I could not feel my skin; I felt death rising upon me. Sydney was facing the wall, my eyes met up with the doctor's as I tried looking out of the window.

"Who's the owner? Is it Joseph or the Holy Spirit?" he mocked and a sharp pain cut down my spine and I felt my eyes blurring. What would he even think hearing the father of my child was none other than my own cousin? I looked down with tears falling down my face. It was all over.

"Travis? I didn't know he was fooling me all this time around. He promised to take good care of you, and I didn't know he meant sleeping with you," good thing he was suspecting Travis, the only option that was left for me was to make people believe that the child in my womb belonged to Travis. It was going to be better that way. 'child in my womb', I could not believe I was the one thinking those thoughts.

"Let me call him, I need to speak with him about this," "Wait! no! It's his of course, you don't need to worry him, and he's at work I'm sure, I'll tell him in due course," I held his hand as he tried dialing a number. He pushed my hand back and dialed the number, when I turned my eyes to ask for Sydney's help, he was not there anymore. I sat down calmly with surrender, knowing Travis was just a few blocks away from where we were. I threw myself back in the chair and gave up on myself. Travis hurried in a few seconds. He stood at the door and smiled as he saw me sitting on the chair, I faked a smile but falling tears betrayed me. He wore a confused face as he saw me crying. He progressed towards me and kissed my forehead sweetly. I wished I would turn the clock back and had my baby owned by Travis, but the milk was spilt and would never be restored.

"What in this world would make my beautiful woman cry? I'm here for you baby, please don't cry," he fondled my cheeks and wiped my tears gently.

"I know you love her much son, but you really shouldn't have, she still has a destiny. She doesn't deserve all this," the doctor said with a disturbed voice, staring at me and then back at Travis.

"What are you talking about Doc?" he asked looking puzzled.

"Trav, let's get out. I need some fresh air," I said as I pulled his hand and tried dragging him out of the surgery.

"No babe! Wait a minute; let's hear what the doctor has to say." I forcefully pulled Travis out with all my power to his surprise and confusion at my behaviors.

"Jay what's wrong with you?"

"Nothing love, I don't need to be in there any longer," I passed through the chair where my mother was seated. She stood up as she saw me and smiled as she saw me with Travis. I realized that if I left my mother seated there, the doctor would see her and tell her the bad news; hence I had to make a plan.

"Mom, everything is fine now, I've been given the medication. May I please stay back with Trav for a few minutes? I'm clean it's confirmed. You may go back home now," I faked a smile and Travis wore a very confused face.

"It's okay my baby, let me thank Mr. Dube."

"No mom, he's...he's busy with someone. Let's just leave, you'll disturb him," mom also looked puzzled but silently obeyed my word, took her bag and left. I breathed as we walked through the corridor and down a green matted lawn. We sat down there, I wished to feel better but the situation was worsening within me.

"Are you okay baby?" that was the first time I felt the sweet sound of his 'baby'. I had thought he was dumb all the time. I saw his handsome face as he tried to smile at me. I felt the gentleness of his warm hands as he touched me. I realized it should have been him who was the father of my child. The whole world was going to be singing happier tunes, even angels in heaven, but how could the spirits, if there be such, celebrate at a girl who disobeyed the laws of humanity that taught to obey our relative's nakedness?

"I'm okay babe, just one of them bad days," I said as I flipped myself and tied my arms around Travis' warm body.

"Whatever it is honey, you can share with me, I'm here for you," he said pitifully.

"Were you serious that you love me Travis?" my voice was shaking.

"What do you mean sweetheart? How could you even ask that? You know I'm insane about you. I can go everywhere, anywhere just to be with you Jay. You're a good girl, every man's dream," he smiled and there was truth and love written all over his face, I wished I was the good girl he pictured me as. I started missing my goodness, I missed it so bad.

"You've been scarce lately, I've been missing you so bad," his voice was dripping honey. I was not completely sure whether it was indeed dripping honey or it was because my mouth tasted bitter at the moment and it was only him who could rescue. I had preferred Sydney's voice to Travis' all the time. I had to be with him for the last time when he still liked me, when the worst page about my life could be opened for him. I lay at Travis chest for the first time and it felt so right to be there, I would not run at the approach of mom, Janet, the doctor or anybody who would see me with Travis. But I would run miles if anybody caught me up with Sydney. He cupped my face with his hand and I tried to smile. I wished God would forgive me right away, cover all my sins from and let me stay with Travis like that for the rest of my life.

"What if you find out that I have flaws, what if I'm not the perfect soul you think I am? Will you still want me?" tears still flowed and I saw his face darkening with curiosity and confusion. He kept quiet a bit and wiped the tears off my eyes.

"Nobody's perfect Jay. I know you have flaws but you have self-control and that's exactly what I like about you," my heartbeat zinged with despair. I had no self-control, if I had it I would not be crying, I would have controlled myself from getting in bed with my cousin. I placed my head back where it was and held onto him even tighter.

"You're behaving so strange Jay and I don't understand the reasons why. Will you even tell me what's wrong with you?" as I raised my eyes and looked behind me, doctor Dube was approaching us, and Sydney was also a few meters away from us headed towards us. Why would that man keep mingling in my business? I hated him for that.

"Trav, please kiss me deeply. Please," I said as I pinned his head down so I could kiss him with tears flooding on my face. He plucked my hand out of his head and cupped my face. "Jay, whatever's stressing you is stealing your brains away from you. Keep calm okay? I'm with you. Breathe and tell me what's going on. I'm confused."

"You shouldn't be confused Travis, you knew exactly what you were doing. You disappointed me to a greater level today, I can't stop thinking about this," Doctor Dube said as he approached us. "Will someone tell me what's going on here?" Travis pulled himself from me and stood up. Sydney showed up behind me, casting an evil eye at Travis, he hated him with passion.

"You believe in God Travis, you're a preacher for that sake. You should've waited until marriage. Sex is not everything, or at least you should've used protection. Now what's all this? What will your church say now that you've impregnated this young girl? She's a role model to all youths in our community, believers and non-believers." Doctor Dube spoke, feeling pity towards me and showing anger to Travis.

Travis' face darkened and I could hear his heart breaking. I sat up with crossed legs on the lawn, powerless and helpless. He stared at me calmly and I heard my heart breaking too. I heard the sounds of blood moving so fast in my veins, I surrendered and looked down, shielding myself from Travis' truthful and Godly eyes. What does evil have to do with goodness?

"Jay sweetie, you are pregnant?" his voice caused streams of tears in my face and I wept so bitterly from the inside. He kept quiet and stared at me, I saw a silent tear running down his cheek and he wiped it away and cleared his throat. Travis' silence, I knew, meant he wanted to defend me from the doctor knowing whose the baby was. His silence meant he took the blame, his heart was breaking and his trust melting away but he still never wanted to show the doctor that the baby was not his, since he read the story through and knew the doctor had no clear answers.

"You're lame you know that?" Sydney roared behind me and directed the question to Travis who silently took the curse and kept his cool. Sydney walked slowly and stood besides Travis and stared at him. "You thought you were going to have chances with her?"

His pertinacious behavior amazed me; he was supposed to be begging Travis not insulting him, begging him to come to our rescue and cover our sins.

"I know you're angry dude, but I love Jasmine. You'll have to understand that someday, I'm tired of you throwing tantrums like a kid every time you see me with her," he stood up for himself.

"He's her cousin and has every right to be angry. You messed up Travis. I trusted you," Doctor Dube came to Sydney's rescue.

"Didn't she tell you the reason why she's crying?" Sydney hated defeat and I hated him with all my insides for that. I pulled him by the hand so we could leave before he destroyed my relationship with Travis but he pushed me hard that I fell on the ground. Travis came to my rescue and helped me up. Sydney blocked his way and held him by the collar.

"She's..." I slithered on the lawn like an angry wounded snake with all my power and managed to get hold of his feet and set my teeth six feet deep on his skin. He let go of Travis and stared down at me rolling on the grass like a snake. I shook my head pleading and begging with him to not tell anything to Travis but his nefarious attitude would not agree with me. He offered his hand to me and helped me stand.

"There's no more time for lies Jay, I won't let this moron here disrespect me," he whispered these words calmly into my ears and I gave up trying to make him understand.

"That's my baby in there; this moron doesn't even have balls," Sydney confessed and I heard my heartbeat clanging loudly, my mind banging, it was over! Doctor Dube nearly fell down, maybe the words made him dizzy.

My embarrassment reached its culminating point, I searched for a zone to lay my eyes at just for that moment. I had broken the trust of a doctor who had believed in me, who had praised me. His eyes were on me, no longer mocking but begging for me to say Sydney was lying. My mouth was wide open and the tears were streaming like a merciless river on my face. I apologized to him with my eyes, searching for a place of refuge. I cursed the thought that tried reminding me of my mother. I saw her call and

I ignored it and looked away. My hands were dancing to a wicked tune and they had no power to pick the call up. I entered the prison and that was the dark paint on my adorned simulacrum.

"What? This is just unbelievable! So you're the one who aroused his feelings on the hospital bed right Jay? How could you? I trusted you, I believed in you. All those prayers, they were empty and fake? what happened? Did he force you?" I closed my eyes and even there heavy guilt still followed me. Even in that darkness I saw every source of my fear- God, mom, Janet, Cheryl, Mercy, the Headmistress, the teachers.

"How could you Jay?" he spoke slowly, I did not answer him. I just gawked at him with my eyes confessing everything to him. He sat down on the lawn and took a long breath.

"I've never been this disappointed in my life, you disappointed me Jasmine."

I tried dragging my weak body like I was inebriated by alcohol to leave the scenario but I fell so hard down the lawn. I was scared of going home; lies were not going to work anymore. I had reached the time of exposure and the games were being left behind. My world was falling apart. That was the end of my reputation and mud was slowly but surely covering my precious name. I had eyes but I could not see, had ears but heard not and the mouth turned to a bowel filling tool rather than of speaking. He breathed. Travis just gawked at me dumbfounded. His eyes took away every glimpse of hope, every ray of light that I had on my relationship with him. He shook his head with disbelief with his eyes and mouth wide open like a scared chameleon and I saw tears running down his face. He was hurt, he was bleeding but I believed his pain was nothing compared to what I was feeling inside of me. I searched for his eyes, for his soul to let me explain that I had failed to resist a temptation, to beg him to take me back and agree to own Sydney's child as his. I could not find his soul; it had sunk deep within my lies. My whole soul was bloody.

"I never ever want to see you near Jasmine again. If I do, I will skin you alive dude. Forget about her and cut every connection you thought you had with her. It was never real," Sydney pointed his finger at Travis as a sign of warning and left us standing there.

"You're so fake it hurts," the Doctor spit on me.

"You're so evil, so inhuman. Your cousin really? Now I understand the reason why you stayed glued to him during his sick days, you had your intentions. At least you got what you wanted," he shook his head.

"I can't believe you fooled me, I can't believe you managed to convince everybody that you're good. I just feel for your mom. A good soul that gave birth to wolves. You disgust me Jasmine; I don't even want to take your name on my lips..." the doctor cursed as he stood up to leave. I was seated there, my dress was dripping wet in the front because of every tear.

"Nobody deserves those words doc, hold your horses. We're all fallible," Travis cried out at the doctor who just stared at him and proceeded walking away.

"I always suspected you guys, but I ignored every thought, I wanted so bad to believe that I was seeing things ,all because of the way I trusted you Jay. I'm still failing to believe this is happening you know," he said. He was weeping for his wasted soul, for his love that was taken for granted, for his image; he had been made cover up, a surface meaning to my deep evil story. I lost my power, my mouth open and my breath running ,away from me. I lost myself on the scenario.

"I'm sorry Travis , I don't know what got to me. I know you hate me now, but I really don't have explanations to this Trav. I'm really sorry," I wept bitterly in front of him.

"I just don't know what to say Jay, give me this space. I need to clear my head, and as for your mom, you need to tell her yourself because her heart will break if she hears this news from somebody else. I'll leave now, get up and go home."   "Do you still love me Tram?" I begged with my teary eyes.

"Just go home Jasmine, I need this space," he stood up, offered his hand and held me up too. He then turned and left.

Defeated, I turned and dragged myself slowly back home, Sydney was long gone and it was unlike him to leave me like that but I understood the game was over. It was time to pay.

CHAPTER ELEVEN

I entered my home grounds as slowly as a nail. I knew I would find mom preparing supper and my slow pace was because I had wanted to find her gone from the kitchen so I could enter freely without irritation, but I heard her humming her favorite church song and I knew something had made her happy- if not seeing me with Travis was. I wiped all the tears off my face as I reached the door and took a long breathe. I was surprised at the absence of my sense of belonging as I entered my own home, my mind was loaded with fear and my head was heavy, my eyes not ready to meet anybody's, especially my mother's. I watched my mom standing there cooking with so much joy. I wished I could greet her with joy like everyday but I had stolen that opportunity from myself and in glimpsing her, tears welled down my cheeks in streams. Trying to imagine how she was going to feel after the beans were spilt to her was like a nightmare, it was unimaginable and completely scary.

"Baby! you're back! I've been waiting for you; I'll kill Travis for keeping you till this hour," she joked leaping up and down like a kitten. I learnt it, something was really causing her hyper. "Anyway, enough about him, you won't believe what I'll tell you sweetheart you won't," tears of joy fell down her face as she sat me down on the sofa.

"You know I'm dying with curiosity right mom?" I managed at last to let my shaking voice out. Mom stopped smiling and stared at me.

"Your condition is worsening, I mean your eyes are red, you've been crying Jay what is it? What did the doctor say? You convinced me everything is alright earlier," I held myself and exhaled loudly.

"I'll be fine mom. Please tell me the good news I might heal," I tried even harder to sound okay.

"Alright baby. I had secretly applied for you to study at the University of Zimbabwe and your application have been approved. My salary has been raised at work, my daughter, your prayers have been answered, and you are finally going to school!" she stood up and shouted so loud that Sydney came out of the room to see what was going on. She danced all around the house.

Instead of joining mom in her joy, I changed the scenario. I tried ignoring a big lump in my throat but could not take it any longer, so I wept. It was loud mourning that my mom ran and held my hand trying to make me sit down.

"Jay baby! what's wrong?" it was obvious my tears were not for joy, I was wailing like somebody was dead. I moved away from her and my weeping grew loud as I held my head with both my hands. Mom stood rigid and confused and hurt too as Sydney tried to make me sit down and keep quiet but I took none of his words and roamed around the whole house weeping very loudly, very painfully, very hopelessly. The tears of sorrow, tears of guilt and regret, the tears one shed when they are tired of their sins and wonder if God would ever forgive them, those tears of surrender, tears of despair, useless tears after the sin has been committed and the consequences has rained down on you. Those were the type of tears I shed.

I went to my mother's bedroom and threw myself hard on her bed; I wept rolling, tossing and turning on them. Going to university had been my every day dream and my mother was working very hard to make sure I attained my goal. It was never easy for her because of her little earnings, I had therefore agreed to take a gap year and let her hustle for me, I was also determined and willing to find a job so I could help her with my school fees however I could not find anything.

I was pregnant and had to stay another year at home without schooling and deep down I knew my mother was going to be hurt to a point of refusing to finance my studies and withdraw her varsity idea.

Mom followed me to her bedroom and sat next to me. My weeping grew so painful and I knew it touched her deep down. I was not sure what to do, confess my sins to her or hide it, mom was an honest being. I thought of telling her myself before she heard the news from someone else.

"What's wrong baby? You're breaking my heart. Please just calm down," she hugged me tightly and I pressed even harder knowing that was the last chance with my mother. I calmed down on her bosom, remembering good days with her and that that day was the end of them.

"Mom, I hope you'll find it in your heart someday to forgive me..."

"Aunt! A neighbor is here to see you," Sydney appeared from nowhere as I was about to spill the beans. Mom put me to sleep with burning curiosity and went out. Sydney came closer to me and gave me an evil eye.

"Do you realize what you were about to do? How could you be so stupid Jay?" he lashed out at me.

"Aren't you the one who told me lies have no room within us anymore? Mom will know it and I feel like it's better if I tell her myself."

"No Jay. Just give her this time, get her for today and enjoy her love while it lasts, tomorrow you'll let her know. This is different from the Travis matter. She's your mother honey," Sydney begged me and I was surprised that he still had the guts to call me 'honey'.

"I don't know anymore Syd, I regret."

"I know it's difficult, I am not at peace myself, but I manage to keep my calm because I don't want to think of the words mom will say if she finds out too."

"We messed up *Cuz*, we really did and the saddest part of this is that there's no turning back. We've betrayed them that believed in us,"

"I know, but we'll be fine someday c'mon Jay," I wished that that 'someday' was that very day I was living in; I was failing to bear the pain.

"I have a plan Jay," Sydney said thoughtfully.

"What is it?" I opened my eyes wider, wishing it was some fruitful idea.

"It's only you, me, Travis and the doctor who knows about this mess and it's a bit easier to keep our parents from going to the hospital right? Let's abort this baby, the same doctor will do it and I'll pay him good money for that. I'll then blackmail him using that abortion thing and that he collected bribery money and you know for that he might lose his job. Nobody would like to lose their job in this chilly situation," I had always been scared of abortions, they were illegal at our church and to me abortion was a nightmare, bribery and blackmail-also illegal and immoral, but I should have thought about all that before jumping to bed with him so I was left with no other choice, as long as all that was going to keep me safe from harm.

"Do you think that will work?" I said, raising my eyebrows and my hopes a bit higher.

"It's worth a try babe and I'm pretty sure it will work."

"Then what do we do to Travis? He's not a person who can be bribed."

"Don't worry about him; I'll take care of him once!" I held my chest and gawked at him.

"What the hell do you even mean by that Sydney?"

"Exactly what you're thinking, I'll kill him. If he's too good to carry other people's secrets then he deserves to die," Sydney said as he stood up and roamed around the house.

"I don't want to be a part of this dangerous game Sydney! Are you also a murderer just like you're a sexual immoral person?" I never knew Sydney was capable of killing, let alone having that thought on his mind. I stood up and held my head with both hands.

"There's a lot you don't know about me baby! You only know I'm capable of impregnating my own cousin, my own uncle's beloved daughter. You only know that I'm a demon, I get to a saint's head and make them devilish, Travis is going to die soon and we're together in this. If the doctor refuses the money he's also going six feet underground. You're already devilish Jasmine, there's no use trying to act all innocent here, I want you to keep your mouth shut till the day you die," Sydney said those words without life in his nostrils, he was devilish, he was soulless and I no longer saw the handsome cousin I was fond of, rather a six-horned beast waiting to consume lives. He was staring into space and smiling to himself and my fear reached its culminating point.

"Sydney baby, I'm sure there's a better way we can handle all this. Please calm down and speak to me, I won't be able to keep all this within me, please sweetie," tears welled down my cheeks as I begged. He turned and gazed at me.

"You own a PhD for keeping secrets Jay, I know that. You've kept secrets for three years now, your mom still think you're a virgin right? You're good at this. I trust you."

"It was a different matter baby, this is just too big, we can keep our baby please," I begged tearfully.

"Evil is evil, it doesn't have sizes. Incest is just as bad as killing, so stop this pretending and maintain your composure my love, we're doing all this tonight. There's no time to waste, I'm leaving now for the doctor, see you in a few minutes," he banged the door and left.

'What have I done? What was I even thinking? Lord forgive me please,' my soul wept as I threw myself hard on the bed and wailed bitterly once again. Sydney was capable of anything, now Travis was going to die and I believed his blood was going to be laid upon me. If I broke the news to mom he was going to skin me alive, I never wanted Travis to die therefore I saw it fit to tell my mother everything before Sydney's arrival, with a made up mind I stood up, went to wash my face in the bathroom and headed towards the kitchen, mom was not there and I was sure she had gone out with whoever had called her. I served myself and sat down, waiting for mom to come back from our neighbor's house so I could humbly confess my sins and apologize.

I switched the television on and tried concentrating my mind on some movies but my mind refused to dwell there, it came back to me and flashed the scenario at the hospital. I held my head with my right hand and even failed to eat my food so I gave up on it, shoved the plate to the sink and went and sat on bed. Mom was taking long, I thought maybe the neighbor knew my story and it was the exact topic they were discussing, I shook with fear.

Sydney rushed in as I was busy with my thoughts and fears, he was breathing heavily a sign that he had been running, and I threw my hands in the air, giving up on confessing my sins to my mother.

"What's the news Syd tell me, did he agree to do the abortion," I stood up and ran to him and he held my cheeks and smiled.

"All sorted sweetheart. He accepted the money and promised to keep his mouth shut and we're going for abortion tonight itself," Sydney said with a glow on his face and I held my chest, my soul hushing a bit.

"Thank you darling, but do you think mom won't suspect anything? All the pregnancy signs are showing through dear, I can't even wash dishes I'm always weak," I said with a worried look.

"She won't have time to suspect you anymore," he said as he sat down on bed. "Why?"

"Because after doing whatever we'll do tonight, we're eloping tomorrow."

"Sydney! No! I'm not going anywhere! If we leave people will suspect us, especially after Travis dies, all this is just wrong Sydney please. You'll go alone, I'm not going anywhere, plus I have to start schooling soon," I wept angrily and he laughed wickedly.

"The foetus on your tummy is my seed remember? As long as it still dwells in your tummy, I call the shots, there's no arguing because you know I hate all that. We're aborting the baby tonight! We're killing Travis tonight, we're eloping tomorrow night. Period. Now get to bed," he raised my chin rudely and gave me instructions like he was Napoleon Bonaparte. I silently obeyed with my soul burning with fear and surrender; I had thrown myself to hell.

"I still love you Jay, We're still going to get married," he whispered in my ear and I pushed him and ignored his words.

The main door swung open and we both knew mom had arrived from the neighbor's house. She sat in the lounge for a few minutes and then progressed towards her bedroom. We kept quiet for almost an hour, after we were sure she was asleep, Sydney shook me up.

"Let's leave now; I'm sure aunt's asleep," I reluctantly woke up, put my shoes on and followed him as he led the way out of our home.

"I'm doing all this because I love you Jasmine, I'm not abusing you. Covering this secret up is better than having the whole world prey on you after you become the victim of guilt and shame. I want us to elope because if I leave you here, you'll suffer and you'll end up blabbering this secret to everyone, at least away there you'll get some fresh air," he said, pinning my hand to his and putting the other on my shoulders.

"You love me?"

"I'll never stop. You're my world Jay," he blocked my way and stopped me from walking.

"I think you're the one who has stopped loving me sweetie."

"I still love you Sydney, I'm only scared."

"I'll be with you till time stands still," he said as he plugged his lips to mine and kissed me. It felt so good to hear that Sydney was with me and still loved me. I felt a bit calm after the kiss.

"Now please calm down sweetie, let's do this without fear, you'll get used to this life now that you're my girl. Forget the police, forget being caught. I and you will be together through everything, I promise you beloved," Sydney begged me, playing with my cheeks.

"I'm calm now honey, now that I've heard you love me and you're doing this for me, I've gathered courage, and I don't love Travis anyway," I said, convincing myself I was safe with my Sydney and he smiled and pegged my lips.

"Now let's go and do this. The doctor said he'll be at his surgery," we moved faster and reached the hospital, through corridors till we got to the doctor's surgery. The lights were on but the door was closed, we knocked and a tall man welcomed us, he was not the same doctor we were looking for.

"Sir, we're looking for Doctor Dube, who owns this surgery," Sydney greeted.

"Oh I'm sorry, he left just a few minutes ago, and he transferred to some hospital out of the country. I'm the new doctor for this hospital now," I nearly collapsed and I saw a frown in Sydney's face.

"So he played with my mind! I'll dig him up; he doesn't know who he is messing with. Now tell us, do you do abortions?" "No, I'm sorry, I don't do that," he stared at me and then closed the door before us and I felt like dying.

"Did you give him the money?"

"No, I had no money, I promised to bring it tomorrow, I phoned mom to send it," he said as we turned back to leave sad and disappointed and Sydney boiling with anger.

"Maybe that's the reason why, but it's good baby that he's away. Our secret is safe now; we won't have to worry about him, only Travis," I comforted him.

"Yeah, that's right. Time to face that opponent, he works a night shift today I gathered some information. We'll attack him at his own desk," Sydney said, dragging me by the hand to Travis' office. He was seated alone there writing whatever he was writing and relaxed, playing gospel music, my heart broke. Sydney dragged me in and Travis raised his eyes which wore surprise at our account.

"How are you guys; I didn't expect to see you. How can I help?"

"Why the hell would we need....?"

"Actually, yeah we need your help, we can't find the doctor we had an appointment with him," I interrupted Sydney, panic attack killing me and Travis put his pen down and stared at us really confused. Sydney cast me an evil and warning eye. "I'm sure you did look at his surgery, he left," Travis said softly.

"I'm not here to play games with you dude, I'm here to give you a serious warning, stay out of my business and you'll be safe and secure. I don't want any rumors spreading about Jay's pregnancy and my affair with her. Now that that coward of a doctor has left, you're the only moron that's left, that might spread the news, if you do that boy; you're definitely going to kiss the ground."

"I don't think by just looking at my face you see a man that gossips, gossip is for women, it's for uneducated people and ungodly people. I'm too special for all that."

"Trav, well, he... he ... we're begging you to keep this to yourself, we'll abort this baby so if you may keep quiet, the news will be buried so easily," I begged and Travis stood up and made an unbelieving face.

"Jasmine you're also into abortion now? What the hell are you even telling me? You're not aborting anything Jasmine, not in my presence, not while I'm still alive," Travis swore and my tears started its habit.

"Of course she'll do it while you're dead and done with!" Sydney pulled the gun from his pocket and pointed it directly at Travis' head and Travis lifted his hands up, a sign of surrender. I felt my pants wetting, I never expected that hell in front of my face.

"Sydney baby! Please sweetheart, don't do this, please honey, please beloved," I begged my soul out on my knees while tears flooded together with urine on the floor.

"My dearly beloved sweetheart, ask for anything and I'll do it please sweetie..." I wailed in a deeply painful way, the way moms wail for their departed children.

"Shut up you silly moron!" Sydney directed the gun at me. "I'll get done with you now; you're one hell of a disturbance in whatever I do."

"No, kill me and leave her alone Sydney, kill me!" Travis rushed and defended me as I begged physically, emotionally and mentally for Sydney to not kill me.

"I've told you a million times to leave Jasmine alone and you won't get that to your rotten sense," Sydney boiled to a hundred degrees Celsius.

"Kill me and leave Jay alone!" Travis tried pushing the gun out of my way to his but Sydney pushed him a meter or two away, the trigger was pulled and the sound of it blocked my hearing sense.

CHAPTER TWELVE

I was home napping on my bed as I woke up, I jumped out quickly and put my clothes on as I noticed Sydney laying next to me, he had his eyes opened staring at the ceiling thoughtfully and immediately my memory started serving me well and flashed the scene of the previous night. I shook with terror once again and he stared at me.

"Travis! where is he? Is he alright Sydney please tell me," I asked teary, praying inwardly that he was alive.

"Where else would he be? mortuary perhaps by now," he uttered sounding unbothered and unshaken.

"No! This can't be, you killed him Sydney! you killed my boyfriend," I wailed and fell down rolling on the floor; Sydney rushed and pressed my mouth shut in anger.

"Shut up! just shut up you silly mouse! you'll get us into trouble with your stupid emotions. We organized this together and we did it, you should be worried about this baby on your tummy right now and not that stupid nerd, he got what he deserved," he warned with a hell of a frown on his forehead, fear gripped me tighter at the thought of Travis' death, a guy who knew the definition of love. Thoughts poured in my head; police, death, mom, church, God, everything haunted me.

For the first time in my life, I thought of suicide, I saw suicide as the only answer for my endless itching questions.

"And Jay, don't ever think of opening your loud mouth to spit a word to anyone, I'll kill you, and not with a gun-I'll strangle you till your last breath with my bare hands, that one I promise," he released his hands from my mouth and I stood up, as frozen as I was and headed towards the kitchen. Sydney was a he-devil not the sweetest cousin I thought he were all the time. How was I going to live with all the thoughts of experiencing someone's death? I moved to the bathroom, poured the water into a bucket and started scrubbing the floor so mercilessly with hurt, anger, regret, guilt, shame and pain victimizing me. I had been involved in a plot to kill someone, not just someone but Travis, who considered me to be his sweetheart. Streams of tears welled down my face. Mom entered the kitchen just as I was busy abusing the floor.

"I wonder what the poor floor did to you that you abuse it this way," shouted my surprised mother as she entered the kitchen, clad in her night gown.

"Morning mom," I did not look into her eyes as my eyes wore tear glasses after I had wiped the tears off them for long and ended ignoring them.

"How are you sweetheart? you were about to tell me something yesterday when your cousin walked in on us, I did not sleep a wink last night, you were asleep when I got back so I didn't want to bother you," I shook with fear remembering the warning I had gotten from Sydney.

"Oh mom, I'm sure it was something silly, because I don't even remember what it was," my eyes still refused to look up and I could not stop scrubbing the floor.

"It must've been something serious that made you wail like you were mourning death of a beloved one, you got me worried. Stop hiding things and tell me what's wrong, I know there's something eating you up, I'm your mother and I can tell when you're hurting," I gave her a side gaze and stared back to the floor wishing to open up to her but failing to and not knowing how.

"Your BP will strike if you worry yourself about unnecessary things mom, just relax, days aren't the same and I'm just a young girl in love, you may be sure there's a lot I face right?" "We used to share everything and I won't tolerate this love if it's hurting you, you're my life Jasmine. If Travis is giving you a hard time then I'll cut him off, I told him too," the mention of Travis name made me scrub the floor with all my energy so as to annoy mom to leave me alone.

"I'm alright mom, stress not," I said after seeing she was never giving me any space to breathe. She shook her head and proceeded to the sink.

"Okay if you say so. Anyway, Aunt Maggie phoned me last night, she's coming over to take Sydney back home. She must be on her way now," the mop I was carrying fell onto the floor, aunt was bad news to me, why would God just watch without stretching His Holy hand to rescue me? "You easily get scared, you break things and you don't even look at me in the eyes anymore yet you say there's nothing wrong with you? You were not even happy with the varsity news, you wailed like a scared puppy," mom cried out with her eyes hungry with curiosity. "You're always worried about unnecessary things aunt, Jay is just overwhelmed," Sydney came to my defense as he entered the kitchen faking smiles, his face made me sick but his defense saved me from hell.

"And you always come to her rescue, always," I shook with fear, mom was noticing everything.

"She's my cousin; I understand her better because I spend most of time with her," he defended himself too.

"I'm sure she's alright, I'm praying she's alright because I don't want anything abusing my daughter while I'm alive. I can take seven bullets for her. She's my heart and my soul," mom said, staring at me with pity and love and curiosity.

"Yeah, she's...she's fine," Sydney bit his lower lip. "Anyway Jay I think that this floor is clean now, go and get your medication now," he held me by the hand and pushed me to the corridor leading to our bedroom. Mom was watching with her hands on her bosom as I led the way to the bedroom.

"Jay, about the abortion plan, we'll leave together to Cape Town and abort there then you'll get back and pursue your studies. This marriage thing, if it will occur, will happen after you're done with schooling."

"I don't think mom will let me out of her sight especially now that she suspects there's something going left with me," I said slowly.

"Don't worry about her, just think of ways to convince you're fine and please stop shaking Jasmine you're making me sick, you're exposing us,"   "I'm tired of everything Sydney, I'm fed up. I'm suffering night and day since I slept with you, you won't expect me to be calm. We killed someone for God's sake. Sleeping with you was just better than killing a soul, that's unforgivable."

"That's the problem with you! Why are you even thinking about God? especially now that you're this wicked? leave God for the holy, you're no longer on that class Jasmine. That guy is dead and you won't ever see him again. He should've known better than to mess with me. I'm Sydney and nobody will mess with me and get away with it, I told him a million times to leave you the hell alone but he thought he was better enough to be on my level."

Pride was written on his face, wicked pride- the pride that destroys. All I thought about was jail, being caught and he was on with his praises for himself. There was a knock on the main door as we were busy with our discussions and I froze thinking maybe it was the police and I was done with. Mom attended the knock and I stood and peeped through the door in need to see whoever it was.

"Maggie," I heard mom scream, aunt had arrived and my headache started.

"Damn it!" Sydney cursed as he heard his mother arriving.

"Laurie, my wife!" aunt screamed back as they shared a cozy tight hug. Mom and aunt shared an unbreakable bond since my dad was alive, even after dad's death, their bond was amazing. They were best friends, mom saw Sydney as her own child while aunt saw us as her own children too. That thought made me sick again, wondering how I was even bedded by my own cousin who was more like a brother to me.

"How are you and the kids? Where are they? I can't wait to see them!" we heard aunt say, I saw Sydney putting on a facade of a happy sweet face and he winked an eye at me to do the same and we progressed towards the kitchen where they were.

"My baby!" she ran and greeted him with hugs and teary smiles and I saw him faking them back at her.

"I'm stronger than before," he boasted. I wished to never be a part of that scenario; aunt progressed towards me and I stood still, failed to fake smiles or laughter, and tears were forming in my eyes and I just offered her a faint hug which left her with questions.

"What's wrong baby look sad. Did Sydney give you any trouble again?" Sydney was busy making signs for me to cheer up.

"At least I'm not the only one who sees she's not herself, I've been asking her what's wrong and she pretends she's alright," mom responded.

"Oh! my poor baby! she'll be fine Laurie; we all have bad days," aunt rubbed my back and kissed my cheeks.

"How are they? are they still enemies?" she laughed as she sat down on the couch and mom joined her along. I was silent, trying hard to swallow throbs and big lumps that stood on my throat.

"The enmity ended the day we scolded her. They're close in a very strange way now, always together, always fighting for each other," a bright smile crossed her face. "I swear they never leave each other's side," she complimented further as if we were not there.

"And did she tell you she ended up with Travis?" mom asked aunt and I coughed so hard, a fake cough of course because my throat was clear, only full of lumps.

"Janet told me before she did! I knew it before I left," aunt laughed and winked an eye at me. I was a dead person's girlfriend and I had to pretend he was alive because Sydney was watching me like a hawk.

"Very good news. I'm happy for you my baby, because soon you'll be his bride, I know he has good intentions,"

"Aunt, aren't you hungry?" I could no longer take it, I stood up.

"Yes baby, I know we're making you blush at the mention of

Travis' name, I know them-goose bumps," she laughed naughtily.

"Just make tea for everybody baby! We all haven't had breakfast yet," mom said as I was already five steps away from them towards the kitchen, running away from the heating flame behind me.

"Anyway mom, I'll be leaving with Jay to Cape Town, she needs to be away from this place for some time," Sydney lashed out and I closed my eyes.

"What? No Sydney, Jasmine is going to school two months from now; I've found a place for her. I'm sorry; she'll visit you guys during the holidays, you never discussed this with me first also," mom said in shock.

"Two months from now, that's way too far, she'll stay for a month only. She will even get groceries and a pocket money aunt please," he begged.

"Let the kids go Laurie, if that's the case then she'll be alright," aunt begged for us.

"You don't know how hard it is for me to stay with Jay out of my sight. These two months I thought I'd be trying hard to get used to the fact that school owns her now," mom said with a look of worry across her face and tears welled down my cheeks and flooded on the sink. A few kids were blessed with mothers like mine. Why didn't I recognize the blessing?

"Let her go for only two weeks then aunt, just two. It'll break my heart to see my sweetheart leaving for school without any money or groceries while I have millions in my bank account," Sydney pretended to be heartbroken. The mention of 'sweetheart' planted unending smiles on aunt and mom's faces as they exchanged glances and Sydney won the battle.

"It's alright dear, you guys can go. Just don't keep her for too long please," mom smiled.

"My brother would be the happiest man alive to see this sweet bond. I love you so much my kids," aunt poured her love unto us with tears filling her eyes. I could no longer hold mine, I was never wiping them away, I let them fall and stream to wherever they saw fit to be. Would my dad be happy that I was pregnant with my cousin's child?

"So when's Travis paying bride price honey?" aunt directed the question to me smiling as she unpacked her clothes. I quickly wiped the tears off my face and exhaled out loud, settling my fears.

"He's...still hustling aunt," I managed to say, hoping I'd say it out that he was dead but fearing the gun that Sydney owned. "Come on! he's from a prosperous family that one; he doesn't need to hustle to get money. I'm sure he's working because he just wants to," aunt flashed her white teeth.

"I'm the happiest woman alive to have him as my son-in-law. He's well-tempered," mom laughed and I wished to put her happiness to a halt at that very moment. It hurt seeing her hopes so high because of my fake character.

"How are my businesses going mom? I miss being there and I need lots of money, did you bring anything for me?" Sydney interrupted the Travis topic intentionally; maybe it was disturbing him too deep down.

"Everything is moving well sweetheart. You'll get the money you need and your employers miss you a lot but no I didn't bring any money with me here, just to take you home," Sydney lived that kind of a life where he had everything he wanted, that was the reason why he was a spoilt brat to an extent of thinking he could wife his cousin without hindrances.

"I'm glad to hear that," he was not his real self and I was the only one who understood the reason.

"Oh and Vuyo sent her regards. She would not stop crying after I told her you had an accident. She even wanted to come with me here," I wondered who that Vuyo was, I was pretty sure it was Sydney's girlfriend.

"Oh! I hope you told her I'm fine," Sydney avoided my eyes and I read into it. That Vuyo was his girlfriend for sure, I did not know why but jealous stroke me so hard.

"Who's Vuyo now Maggie?" mom asked as she was as curious as me.

"It's my daughter-in-law Laurie, Sydney's girlfriend. She loves him a lot, she's not been well since he came here," I inhaled some hot air, so he had a girlfriend for real.

"Oh! I've never heard of her, he didn't tell me," mom smiled. "We're proud of you Syd; you really should pay bride price. We don't want any pregnancy before marriage," I nearly collapsed hearing those words coming out of my mother's mouth. Sydney tried saying something but he also swallowed his words.

"I'll go to rest a little bit in my room mom, call me if you need anything." I said after being done with the dishes.

"Alright baby, take these groceries to my room, we'll unpack them later," I did as I was told and went and threw myself to bed. I needed time to be alone and meditate upon my mistakes. Sydney broke in just before I could start thinking.

"I'm sorry I didn't tell you about this Vuyo thing, I should've told you," he placed his hand on my stomach, I pushed it away.

"We should stop all this Sydney, we're cousins and it should feel like it. I was the stupid one here and I don't think it's all about who has Vuyo or who doesn't. This thing is between us," I spoke tearfully and angrily.

"You should've known you are my cousin long back before you asked me to sleep with you, Jasmine, we need solutions here you can't back down now that's impossible, we've already been through a lot together," he would not repent from his nefarious voice and spirit.

"You're going crazy Sydney, don't you see you are abusing my emotions?" our voices went beyond mere whispers as we started throwing tantrums at each other.

"Shut the f** up you silly moron! Do you want them to hear us?" he nearly slapped me and I dodged his hand and fell onto the bed. He had gathered too much power wanting to slap me hence fell on top of me. We were both angry and my chest was burning so hard. He stared at me slowly and I stared back at him remembering the lustful days I had had with him. His eyes slowly cooled and he bent down to kiss me, maybe I needed to kiss him too hence I wrapped my hands around his steel body. I closed my eyes and welcomed his lips as he dipped them vigorously into mine. The kiss had just begun as the door swung open and he rolled and slept next to me and pretended to be dead asleep. I exhaled some fiery hot air, I was a real moron. Mom barged in and looked at us curiously.

"What's wrong with you two? What is always wrong with you two? for God's sake?" she sat on the bed and watched Sydney pretending to snore.

"Nothing serious mom," I faked a smile.

"Okay then, he's pretending to be dead asleep this one," mom laughed. Sydney opened his eyes and laughed too.

"Well, let me leave you to it then. I just hope you're not back to your old habits," she left us and Sydney got back to me. I pushed him hard and he squeezed my hand tight.

"We were about to kiss and your mom interrupted us Jay c'mon I want you right now."

"You smoke *nyaope* you moron! how could you be so immature?" I freed my hand from his and left the bed to the wardrobe.

"Tomorrow we're leaving," I started packing his clothes. "Yes baby, we are. I can't wait to stay alone with you where I'll be eating you up without fear," he smirked and I frowned.

"Shut up Sydney!"

It would be better if I phoned my mother from Cape Town and told her the news than telling her live.

I knew I was soon going to be the talk of the town and I had to run away from it. I thought him being away would give me some space and would not raise any suspicion on our parents but deep down I knew I was never going to handle things well alone. We moved to the lounge where mom and aunt were seated chatting and I took the way to the kitchen. I took beef from the fridge and started cutting it for relish. I was so relieved by the thought for leaving to Cape Town and leaving my sins behind hence I was smiling, the sour mood was gone. Sydney was happy too and laughing out loud at the lounge with mom and aunt. I was going to live with my cousin and get married to him without any tension.

"Why are you happy all of a sudden?" mom asked me as I approached them after placing the relish on the stove.

There was a knock on the door just before I could answer her question. I went and opened the door and the man who had challenged us about my good character at the hospital walked in, still wrapped in animal skins and bands. I stood at the door and stared at him, what he would want at my home, I wondered, he had never stepped there.

"Won't you let me in young one?" he smiled and showcased his yellow teeth.

"Who's it Jay?" mom came and saw the man, aunt followed her too and she frowned as she caught a glimpse of him.

"You? what do you want here? get lost," aunt said, closing the door before the man.

"Wait! Calm down ma'am I come in peace. I'm here for a different mater today. I swear I won't cause any trouble," he looked a little humble and we ended up letting him in and sat him on the couch. I served everybody breakfast, including the man and went and joined Sydney on the couch and the man stared us and smiled, I just rolled my eyes, my heart remembering every word he had said.

"I see your son has healed completely ma'am," the man said to aunt laughing after the greetings and pouring tea into his cup.

"Of course he didn't die like you wished him to," aunt said angrily.

"I'll repeat that I'm here for peace ma'am. I understand that you're still angry with me concerning your daughter. I apologize for the words I said, the truth always wins and I'm here for that," I looked down at the mention of truth.

"Alright, what are you here for? Maybe you're here for our tea since you came during our breakfast," aunt bit her lower lip smiling mockingly and the man just smiled.

"I have enough food in my home but I still like eating with other people," he said, sipping hot tea and making funny sounds.

"What are you here for?" mom asked in annoyance.

"Oh! I'm not here with good news, it's some heartbreaking news!" he wore a sad face and I exhaled loudly, Sydney cast a glance at me. I smelled trouble coming my way and I sat up straight wishing with all I had I was never the bad news he was bringing to my family.

"What bad news now? One of your children disappointed you again?" aunt mocked once again.

"You may put it like that, but my children won't concern you I guess. One of your children is in a broken state right now," I felt fear forecast on my soul and I stared at the man with begging eyes. "What the hell are you even talking about? You said you're here for peace and now you're on with your nonsense?" Aunt was gaining the heat; her flipping forehead told me that. "Sir, do you maybe need some more tea?" I stood up and hurried to him, I knelt before him, wishing the heavens could shut his big mouth. He could not see he was tearing my world apart. Mom was reading too much to my strange actions. I signaled to him to never say a word but he ignored me like I was some morsel of dust in the cosmos.

"No thank you dear, I still have some in my cup," he rudely smiled showcasing his aged brown teeth and I closed my two golden globes with surrender. I slowly marched towards my space like a scared dog. Sydney shook his head signaling that I was not supposed to fret. I got a little hope, seemed like he had everything under control.

"I know and everybody knows yesterday's incident that befell your nurse son-in-law, I'm therefore here to pass my heartfelt condolences to this family. I know he is your favorite, I heard he's dating your beautiful daughter here," he sadness and pity in his face, I read into the matter, Travis death news had spread to the whole town. Mom stood up, dying with curiosity.

"Stop beating about the bush! Just go straight to the matter," she roared.

"I'm very sorry ma'am, tradition has it that you have to respect some news, you just don't say them out like that."

"I'm sure you're not here to teach us about tradition! Our parents taught us that way back before your teeth got this brown!" aunt insulted.

"He's making me sick!" mom spit.

"Jay, what happened to Travis? Didn't he call you? Is he alright?" I trembled with fear and a silent tear streamed down my face.

"No mom, the last time we spoke, he was fine."

"Then why are you crying? Do you believe this witch? I'm pretty sure he has bewitched my beloved son-in-law. Why are we even keeping him here? He has had enough tea, now leave! Get up and leave! we're tired of your mind games." Aunt stood up and slowly but dangerously headed to the man.

"Wait! Please! I'll speak now! Wait a minute. I'm not the enemy here, Travis was shot yesterday night at the hospital..."

"What? Is he alright?" mom covered her mouth with both her hands and shed a tear. Mine streamed like a loaded river and I did not bother wiping them away. I was clad with unexplainable guilt, the mountainous guilt that puts all its weight over you.

"He was badly hurt but luckily by the grace of God, he survived, the bullet didn't touch the heart and other sensitive organs," the man said pitifully and Sydney opened his eyes wide hearing Travis was not dead, I took a deep breath, thanking God for saving him, I thanked God that Travis was saved and I was not a murderer.

"Who would do such a thing to him? why would they do it? Where were the police? why wasn't the damn killer caught? the killer must rot in jail! this isn't like our country, we rarely hear gun stories and all! I'm sure the killer must have come from South Africa!" aunt said in sobs, he loved Travis with all her heart. I shook with terrible fear.

"It's really heart breaking. I don't know how some people could be so evil. This is the definition of evil. We've never heard of such things in this place," the man said as he took a sip of tea and my tears could not stop welling down my cheeks. Mom and aunt stared at me pitifully; I knew they saw my tears and thought I was weeping for Travis. "Jay, I'm really sorry my daughter. He's going to be fine. Please don't worry he'll be fine," mom came and rubbed my back, hugging me tightly. I prayed she did not come to know the truth. I did not hug my mother back. I felt too numb.

I sat on the sofa searching for a place to hide, a place of refuge. "What if the murderer is in the family? People are wolves in sheep's clothing,"

I gathered all the information from his looks at me, my heartbeat changed, that man knew something!

"I think the time for you to leave has come, you are starting with your stupid accusations and your lies, get out!" aunt growled and the man clapped.

"That's one problem with you guys, you think you are one perfect family who have raised perfect children when your kids are nothing but rotten! There's a lot going on under your roof that you don't know about yet you act all aggressive and holy on me!"

Mom stood up and her eyes roamed around the whole house, to me, to the man and to aunt as she was trying hard to find answers. I was already crying and Sydney had his head laid on the sofa prepared for anything, I also surrendered my soul to the devil and wept.

"I told you that the day will come when you'd remember my words from the hospital, that no one is flawless, that these teenagers are evil as hell, now I'm here to ask you where my lies are?"

"Sydney stop him please, stop him cousin please…" I wept my lungs out on Sydney's laps, but he whispered back.

"Let him talk my love, let the truth come out, it's high time it did. Let's face this,"

"The ancestors have shown me…"

"We don't believe in such things. We believe in the true Living God not these ancestral things of yours, get out!" mom screamed at him.

"God?" the man giggled. "For sure you believe in God that's why there's some incest going on under your roof. That's why your Holy Mary that you defended like that in the hospital is sleeping with her own cousin! I wonder what crooked god is it that you believe in…"

The moment caught me, where I wished I was deaf and blind. I wished I had never read the Holy Bible and heard of a thing such as sexual immorality. I wished I had never been taught about God. I wished He was a new thing. I wished the earth could open up and swallow me alive and I could disappear.

What cut through me cannot be explained as pain, pain would be a small word to describe what I felt at that moment. My mother's eyes grew wide with shock. The man's eyes were on me and my aunt's eyes also on me. Why would they worry about Sydney? They all knew who he really was; it would have not been surprising to them to hear that Sydney had murdered somebody because they all knew he was a bad boy. I was the monster there, the cause of all badness.

"What?" I noticed my mother's face changing slowly to that of an angry dog. She looked as if she would growl, as if she would bite me. The skin in her forehead was forging like a newspaper with the scariest frown I had ever seen. She was bitter and was about to eat me alive.

"No, this is not true Jasmine, right Sydney?" aunt asked.

"It's very true!" the man continued. "Your son is the one who shot Travis last night in an attempt to kill him, because he doesn't want him near his cousin who is also his sweetheart. What an interesting story!"

"I'm sorry mom, I'm sorry, " I knelt down in front of her and a hard, heated slap came across my face and glued me with the wall. I fell with my stomach and I rolled and tossed on the floor in unimaginable pangs of agony. She roamed around the house with her hands on her head, spitting to the floor, starring at Sydney who just laid his head on the sofa and looked at the ceiling unwavering.

"She's pregnant you should not beat her up like that, she'll miscarry," I confirmed that the man was truly some magician, how did he get to know all that information?

"Pregnant? who's pregnant...? Sydney what the hell? what did you do my child?" mom lamented and aunt joined her, they both held her heads with her hands in utter stupefaction. Sydney was silent all the time while I was rolling on the floor holding my cheek where mom had slapped me and my other hand rubbing my stomach; I was in great pain and mourning bitterly.

"What do you want to know mom and aunt? Yeah, she's pregnant with my child, it's all true, we did it. I love Jasmine and I would like to marry her," Sydney said without any fear or hesitation. He sounded relaxed.

"Jay baby tell me this is a worst nightmare and I'm going to wake up my child please tell me. Tell me it's all lies they're just jealous of your goodness please baby. Jay you're my only hope, my pride you're everything baby tell me it's all lies," I had never felt so much pain in my life. I felt my heart beating in slow motion and my eyes went blind while they were wide open. My own mother had her knees on the floor begging me to comfort her like every day; she was begging me to tell her something that would sound like music to her ears, but there was nothing harmonious that would come out of my stained mouth. I had ceased being a nightingale and became an owl the very day I chose getting into bed with my own father's nephew. I felt like I was the definition 'sin' itself. Janet had caused mom's sorrow but it had never reached the extent of mom weeping that loud, mourning and begging that sorrowfully. Aunt stood in rage, her anger I could see written in her face as she grinded her teeth and shook her mouth left and right, she too was sweating and her huge body was cursing. Her stomach was moving up and down as she exhaled and inhaled loudly.

"I've sinned mom, I did! I lost my virginity at the day of my ordination, that…."

"Oh my God! What am I hearing with my own ears? Jasmine oh Jasmine my baby," mom wept, it was high time I confessed, there was no more room for lies.

"That's why you always fought with Sydney? That was all fake? You've been sexual active for year's Jasmine?" aunt screamed in utter shock.

"Yes aunt I have, I've been sleeping with my cousin ever since, he said he loved me, he said he wants to marry me, I believed him. I didn't love Travis, he was a cover up…"

"Shut up!" mom screamed on top of her lungs and I continued weeping and lamenting.

She stood up and headed towards her bedroom and locked herself in there. I followed her with my eyes and wished death could swallow me. I remembered one of the statements I had heard at the Bible study group that said; 'What do you do when your heart is broken by your healer.' I was supposed to be my mother's healer but I had failed to do my job. I had played the game but broke all the rules. Aunt went and took a belt in our room, it was Sydney's belt. I could not run away, I was stuck on the floor, the guilt was heavy I was failing to lift it from my shoulders and my stomach was burning so severely. Sydney stayed too. We both looked at her thinking she wanted to scare us but it was never like that. She grabbed me with her hand and whipped me like I was some kind of a donkey. I could not remember the last time I had been beaten that much. She did hit Sydney too but he pulled the belt from her and went out of the house before she could reach four whips. I was left alone with her, I had been hit so hard that I could not move or sit. I lay there helpless with blood oozing everywhere, from my mouth, nose, and all the bruises all over my body. I feared the baby would die because my stomach had bruises too. The other part of me wanted it to die but the other part wished for its life. The man could not stand the heat in the house and left. I remembered the words he had told mom and aunt and how they had convinced him that I was an angel.

"You're disgusting Jasmine. You're very cunning and I believe you dragged my son into this. You couldn't resist his handsomeness. You lied about Travis. You made all of us believe in you, you begged for me to leave Sydney behind when you had your evil intentions on him," she was shedding tears and she was red with anger. I vowed to not reply a thing to her so I let every curse over me settle through me, I felt like I deserved every curse. The guilt in me had made me so humble that I accepted everything with total acceptance. Mom walked in slowly, sat on the sofa and cast a glance of disgust at me. I had never seen such a face on her; even Janet had never pained her to that extent.

"So you're the one who aroused him at the hospital bed right?" she asked. I looked down and nodded, feeling the pain from every side, from my body, my heart and my soul.   "Jay I never thought you could do this. You've betrayed me. I believed in you, I loved you from the core, even now I'm still trying hard to believe what I heard but I can't. I never have felt this stupid before. You lied about everything, you painted us with mud, you stopped going to church because you wanted to remain behind indulging in sexual activities with Sydney? I can't believe this. I'm failing to believe it's you my daughter. You're a real witch. There's nothing more badly than you in this world. You're evil. I hate you, I disown you from today onwards never call me your mother and I'll never address you as my daughter. I've come to realize how better Janet really is. She has shown me disrespect openly and she has boyfriends but never see her cousin as a husband material. I don't want to see you here anymore. You'll see where to go. I'm just feeling pity for myself. I wish I had stayed barren. I wish I was a celibate," her last words corroded my soul with a heaviest weight. I felt a piece of my heart falling. I felt my lungs stop supplying oxygen, I was the reason my mother was wishing she had stayed barren. My mind was flooding and I was slowly getting tired of everything. I sat up and leaned my head and my body against the wall. She spat on my face and turned to leave. I did not bother wiping the saliva on my face. I deserved every piece of hell they gave me. The door swung open just before my mother could leave.

"The whole school knows! Jay how could you? You?" it was Janet and Cheryl. My day was completely cursed; God was completing His mission of exposing me. Cheryl was smiling mockingly at me and mom stopped to look at them.

"You're my sister; you've always taught me everything about self control, what happened to you Jay? The teachers are disappointed in you. The Headmistress is totally angry at you and now you've also turned me into a laughing stock too. I can't believe this Jay. I'm bad yes, but I would never sleep with my cousin, let alone being impregnated by him. Jay I can't believe it? I remember every time I caught you guys together it was suspicious, you guys pretended to not get along, how long have you been sleeping with our cousin Jay?" I kept my mouth shut as my little sister poured all hell unto my soul. I looked down throughout, I had no power to raise my eyes and look at her. I had always judged her whilst I failed to remove the log in my own eye.

"It's the reason why she denied me the chance of sleeping with Sydney. She probably is the one who called her mother on us, wow I can't believe this! You thought you'd never be caught? She was pretending she was protecting him whilst she knew she wanted him for herself. How cunning your Godly woman is? She even stopped going to the Bible study lessons ever since Sydney came here. She was having a time of her life, poor Travis, he had thought he found himself a trophy. Jasmine you are evil," Cheryl was laughing out as she said those words. My eyes were glued to the floor as I swallowed all the scourges down my soul. I had no choice; I was going to deal with them later. I deserved them, they were not lies. I had done everything to be with Sydney, thinking it would stay a secret not knowing that God says 'there's no hidden thing that will not be put into light'.

"I found them together in bed just a few minutes ago, heaven knows what was being done in my house. I wish my Jack was alive. I can't bear this all alone, I'm broken," the mention of my father's name shattered me into pieces. I wished there was a knife or any sharp object near me so I could just jilt my throat and perish, but there was nothing. I was certain that God wanted me to suffer every pang so I could learn a lesson. I saw death in my mother's face, death of her love, her hopes, and her trust on a mere human being, I saw it all fade away.

The only thing that scared me the most was my mother disowning me because I had nowhere to go. Janet was staring at me, she was angry at me, feeling pity for me and also in doubt that I was the one who did that. Cheryl turned to leave still making a mocking face towards me, I knew she was going out to spread the news to my other friends and make me a laughing stock. Mom and aunt marched together to their bedroom with the tremendous incredulity and disappointment ever. I was left alone with Janet and there was too much pressure and tension, she was gazing at me shaking her head, pinching her skin as if she wanted to check if she was in a real world or was merely dreaming. My heart was beating too fast and I was slowly losing my energy and pretty sure my time of death had approached. My eyes blurred slowly and I fell hard to the floor with my forehead. I lost my consciousness.

CHAPTER THIRTEEN

I was dressed in a light blue hospital gown as I opened my eyes. There were two drips attached to my hands, the other was a blood drip and the other a water drip,. I was laid in a single bed and I was so weak. I turned my head to look around the house and there was my little sister holding and playing with my fingers. There were tears in her eyes and she was looking at me sorrowfully, her face changed quickly as she noticed me staring at her, she stood up and held me even tighter.

"You're awoke finally sis, I've been praying," she managed to flash a bright smile even in tears.   I smiled back at her.

"What happened to me Jenny, why am I here? where is mom?" she tried smiling but could not fake it.

"You had fallen unconscious sis, I was scared. I could not get any sleep last night I thought you were dead, but here you are," she rejoiced ignoring my other questions but I repeated.

"Where is mom Jenny?" she looked down sadly. My voice was too slow and too low and my whole body was aching.

"Mom is at home sis, she could not come. She's still mad at you but she'll be fine just give her some time," she looked anxious.

"Mad at me? what did I do? mom will never be mad at me?" I had lost my memory but as I closed my eyes, everything came to life like a bright flash of lightning. I remembered everything I had done and the pain and the guilt came and clouded me once again. I wished I could have lost my memory forever but when God punishes you, He makes sure you suffer every consequence of your action so that you will never repeat the same sin again. It was a good chance for me to open up to my little sister, maybe the wounds could heal, I thought. The tears could not fall; I flashed a sorrowful smile and looked at my sister.

"I failed all of you Jay. I know and I'm embarrassed from the deeper core. I'm scared at what the world thinks of me now." "Nobody's perfect sis Jay. I don't support anything you did but I understand that temptations are everywhere," she was a truthful person; she could tell you the truth without the fear of what it could do to you.

"You've always been real. You've always lived your life. You were supposed to be my mentor, not the other way round. I remember that day of my ordination when you told me you were scared for me, I never knew this day would come but here it is, I'm so afraid to say you told me so," a silent tear fell at last and she wiped it off with her hands. "I know its hard sis but you should not give up on yourself now, you have to fight this battle and win or else you'll die. Be strong, there's, you'll hear more blasphemy, feel the worst pain but try hard to pull yourself together. I'm with you in this, I'll never forsake you," she hugged me and I felt safe in her arms, it made me realize how strong she was and the hidden power she had inspired me.

"Thank you Jenny, I kind of know I'll be fine, but I know it won't be anytime soon. My dreams are shattered, my world has fallen apart and I have ruined my own reputation and painted it with a dark color. I've failed my mom, she's done nothing but loved and believed in me, but what did I do?"

"You cannot go back and undo what you've done sis, now try hard to accept your mistakes, meditate on them and move on." "Thank you dear for motivating me. It's still hard but I'll go on," I said all those words hoping and praying that I could be alright even though I knew it would take time. A gram of weight was lifted off my shoulders seeing my sister was on my side and I was never alone. Janet could never fake her love for me, if she was mad at me, she would show it. Deep down her I knew she was angry with me but she did anything to make sure I was safe and secure. I could not blame her for being mad at me or anyone, I only had myself to blame. I remembered the preaching at church by Travis, when he said, 'There's no pain in this world more painful, more disturbing, more killing than the pain you cause to yourself without anybody to blame. Guilt corrodes your soul, shame washes off all your self-esteem and embarrassment drowns you in the deepest sea of loneliness. Pain itself is unbearable. That's the kind of pain people to cause to themselves by disobeying God and succumbing to temptations.' That was the kind I went through, everything valuable to me was wasting away in front of me and I could do nothing but watch.

"Tell me what happened really? How did Sydney drag you into doing this sis? I hate him with all my insides," she frowned.

"We're both to blame Jenny. Remember that ordination night when he escorted me back home? He seduced me and I fell for it, that was when he broke my virginity."

"Wow? I noticed your mood changes all of a sudden that night, so that's where it all began? It makes sense, the sheets being washed, you not wanting to be ordained all of a sudden."

"Yes little sister, all those times I pretended to hate him, I was just trying to hide my feelings for him. I thought it would make me forget about him. I even prayed about it but I failed to resist him. So when he came back, we continued with our thing, we had sex almost everyday," it was hard confessing but it was better than pushing it all in.

"We kissed at the hospital by the time he was sick. I'm that girl who aroused him. We were nearly caught so we promised to stay away from each other. He obeyed the rule that's why he fell for Cheryl; he was trying to distance himself from me. I fought because I was failing to be away from him," I was crying as I noticed how easily I had succumbed to a temptation without second thoughts or self control. My little sister was listening to me with disbelief, especially to that part that had disgusted her most: arousing him on his sickbed but still, she hugged me and comforted me as I confessed in sobs.

"It's alright Jay, it all will pass. Just believe in yourself," she was crying too.

"I'm scared Jenny, scared of everything. How will people look at me now?"

"Don't worry about them, you're the center of attraction for now but it will be over soon," I wished somebody could kill someone so they could take my place of being the centre of attraction. "Was the foetus hurt?" I changed the topic.

"No sis, he's alright," she smiled seeing I was gaining my confidence.

"He?" I asked in shock and Janet chuckled.

"Yes sis, it's a boy. The doctor did a scan, I thought you were dying, so I asked the doctor to check the baby for me and if there's any way he could survive I would keep him," she was smiling and I smiled back. I was relieved and pained at the same time. I had dreamed of having a boy as my first born but I never wanted it to have my cousin as its father. I remembered I had been disowned.

"Jenny, mom disowned me, said she doesn't want to see me at her place anymore. Where will I go from here?"

"She said those words out of anger dear, maybe she will calm down."

"I hope so dear. Has aunt gone back to Cape Town?"

"No she was there with mom when I left."

I spent the day chatting with my little sister, she was trying so hard to make me feel better and I was also trying to forget about everything. I gained my strength and my consciousness and the doctor came and discharged me.

"You're well now, you may go back home but sadly your mother is in a worst condition. Her BP is very high, she can't talk, eat or breathe, she's in a coma and we doubt her survival. I'm sorry," he gave me the pills and left. Things I saw on movies or read about in novels were happening in my real life, it was like a worst horror movie playing on television. My mother was dying because of my sins. My little sister held on tightly to me. She had been dragged to that spot because of my sins. I had to try and be strong for her. I sat on the bed as she wept sorrowfully. I had caused pain to the whole family, to my mom's friends and everyone who believed in me, my sister was getting dragged into that whole mess, she was losing a mother, and my mother was dying because of me.

"This is too much Jay it's too much!" she wept bitterly and broke the piece of my heart that had been left clinging after my exposure.

"I know and I'm sorry Jenny, may we go and see her please," we dragged each other to the room where my mom was admitted.

We peeped inside, I saw my mother lying lifeless in the bed, and the oxygen machine was fitted on her nose and mouth. I stood like a statue not knowing what to do. I was the only reason my mother was in that heartbreaking condition. My sister pushed me inside and we rushed to her bed. A well of tears found their way down my cheeks and I joined my sister and we mourned together.

"Mom, come back to us please. We need you. We...we...we ...are nothing but dogs, and demons that disturb your peaceful world mom but we promise you a safer place when you come back to life please mom..." Janet wept in a very painful way, I had never seen her so humble before. I never knew she loved mom that much.

"Mom, I know...that I'm the last thing you want to see or hear right now, but please may you find it in your heart to forgive me someday. Mom you're in this bed of anguish because of me. I've broken every hope within you and I know what I have done is the most disappointing thing a child could do to their parent, but mom I confess all my sins to you right now. I am sorry; I'm very sorry mom. I wish I had a chance to undo what I have done. Forgive me please," I poured my whole soul to her, wishing she could hear me and understand that I regret every single thing I had done. I wished she could see how ashamed I was of my actions.

"Jenny let's pray," we bowed our heads and I started a prayer. "Father, in the name of Jesus Christ I come before You now, I understand Lord that I'm the dirtiest thing in Your Holy eyes right now. I accept every punishment upon me Jehovah but may You please stretch Your Holy hand and touch and heal my mother Lord. Please don't pour Your wrath on her too; Lord put every punishment on me. Lord I've tarnished Your name and people are starting to believe You're not the true God. I've led astray every child that had me as their role model. I've made Your church's name ruined too. Nobody believes me now, people doubt You now because of me, but with You Lord there isn't nothing impossible. Give me the second chance to prove to my mom that You live Jesus and You rejoice over a repented sinner like me. I believe she will woke up Jehovah, I believe Your Holy hand is upon her now Jesus. Thank You Father because You've already heard my prayer and granted me everything I've prayed for. In the name....."

"Get the hell out of this room!" aunt hurried over to me, grabbed me by the collar of my dress and threw me out of the room just before I could say amen.

"Don't come here with your stinking ass and pretend to be holy. We know you now, don't ever dare set your dirty feet over here or else I'll kill you with my bare hands. You think God hears hypocrites like you, bastard! I'm starting to question whether you're my own brother's son. You're saved by the fact that your mother is not a prostitute like you. Now get lost! Your mother told me to never let you near her bed, who knows, you might poison her since you're a dangerous serpent..."

"Aunt stop!" Janet shouted from behind.

"My mother is in here battling for her life and you're busy throwing allegations to my sister. She's no perfect soul just let her breath at once!" she said angrily. I was dumbfounded and hurt by every word that aunt had thrown at me. I needed to leave.

"I don't care about anything you say Jenny, your sister stinks, you won't pretend as if she's not the reason why Laurie is in this condition right now," "What does she even want here?" mom's friend, that nurse who used to like me so much asked.

"Her mom's BP is so high, her presence will worsen it. She should leave now."

"Yes this kid must go!" the neighbor of ours was there too.

"You're disgusting Jasmine. You really are."

"She needs to be expelled from our church. She has ruined our reputation we believed in her. She has been stopped to attend church from today," I noticed the congregation from church and I gathered courage to just stand and listen to every curse upon me. I failed to look at them; I had really spilled myself with chili sauce, everything became bitter. Janet tried with everything she had to defend me but she failed. I was chased out of the hospital. I stayed just nearby the hospital and prayed to God to help my little sister. It was over for me but I was still feeling pity for Janet, it was my entire fault that she was losing a mother too. My head was pounding with unanswerable questions; heaven knows where Sydney had disappeared leave me in such unimaginable anguish. I was sitting on a rock alone with my thoughts, praying, and crying all at the same. I heard a hand touch my shoulders turning me around, it was Travis. He was completely well thank God, I did not look at him in the eyes; I just stole a single glance at him and looked down.

"For how long will you stay here? You need to be thinking about where to sleep tonight," I did not understand what was in his voice, pity or mockery.

"I still have a home."

"That's what you think? I have opposing evidence here with me. Look behind you," I obeyed him and turned around to look behind me, there was my suitcase, and a plastic bag with shoes shabbily packed. I knew it was my aunt who had done that.

"Who brought them here?" I asked with my low, pained voice.
"Your aunt brought them and she sent me to give you."

"Thank you," I pulled them near me and leaned on them. I waited forward for Travis to leave my presence. It was so humiliating having him there standing there seeing a girl who had played hard to get on him while getting showed by her cousin, suffering that way. He stood behind me as I sat there praying he could leave.

"But what really happened to you Jay?" he was never leaving. "I failed you. I'm not who you thought I was, may you please leave me alone for now,"

"I'm sorry, so where are you going to sleep?"

"I'll see. I'll go and try my friend Mercy," I got off the rock and placed my head on my suitcase. I told myself that was where I was going to sleep overnight since it was already dusk. I was never sure of how I was going to face Mercy but I had to try somehow. Part of me wanted to go with him but I knew he lived with his parents and I was not ready to meet any church member in that situation. I had to wait for him to leave so I would go and try Mercy.

"I can offer you a place for tonight if you don't mind," "No don't worry about me, I'll be fine here and thank you," he begged me further but I would not agree to his offer. He left after trying hard. A few minutes after he was gone, I sneaked away to Mercy's place. It was dark and I was scared but I knew she was not sleeping, she usually slept late. Mercy's mom was a humble soul and I knew I was going to be welcomed with warm hands. I was a bit scared of their reactions but I managed to gather some courage and knocked.

"Who's there?" It was her mom's voice and I trembled with fear hence I did not reply. The door swung open before me and my eyes met up with Mercy's. She stood still and stared at me.

"Ohh! You! How are you? It's been long," there was no friendliness in her voice rather mockery. I read them pages of a closed book.

"I'm okay. I need your help," I said with a low voice.

"How can I help you?" she was standing on the doorway holding door like she was going to bang it on me.

"I need a place to sleep for tonight; mom has shown me out of the door," I begged.

"Do you somehow blame her?" It was not a good time for me to be answering those kinds of questions considering the fact that I was in deep pain. I shook my head unwillingly and frowned a little.

"Where is Sydney? He should know he's responsible for this. Where is he?"

"I don't know," he was the last person I needed to be questioned about at that condition, I knew her purpose was to sink deep the needle in me and she performed it very well.

"So you came here thinking I was going to pity you and keep you in? No sis listen, Cheryl is my best friend and you know it, she told me everything that happened, all the accusations you threw on her when you knew you were the one who was busy sexing your cousin behind her back, how will I know you won't end up stealing my boyfriend too? There's no place for wolves in sheep's clothing here darling," she was about to close the door when her mom appeared behind her.

"What does she want here? I don't want her near you anymore, gosh she has nerves showing up on my doorstep," she shouted.

"Please leave my compound; my child has nothing to do with prostitutes like you," I had never pictured Mercy's mother as that type of a mother but I did not blame her though, I was a nuisance to the world at that moment. She closed the door before me. I rolled my mouth and stepped back embarrassed. All my friends had turned their backs on me, my relatives and the community as a whole but I had never thought Mercy could be so rude to me. After realizing I had nowhere to set my head on, I slowly marched back to the rock where I had left my clothes. My body was walking but I was no longer sure whether I was alive or not.

The shame that covered my soul, the thick darkness of guilt took over me. I was crying but I knew it was useless; tears would have never solved my problems. As I approached my spot, a hurting surprise hit me hard on the nerves; my clothes were no longer there. I searched everywhere trembling and shaking with fear but my suitcase was nowhere to be found. It dawned on me that God punishes people who drag His name through the mud, people who pretend to worship Him while their sins lurk dangerously on their minds and hearts. I folded my body near the rock and tried hard falling asleep. The chill dealt with me so adequately during the night. I could not close my eyes in fear of any beast attacking me, I did not know when I faded off to sleep.

****

I woke up exhausted, hungry and tired. My bag was not with me and I did not know where to search hence I understood I was the prey of all the night beasts. I never stopped praying for mom to heal and my sister too even though I was their worst opponent at that moment. I was worried about the soul in my womb, how was he going to survive? Pregnant people need proper food, shelter and comfort. My distress was never good for my little unborn spirit and I had to try to be strong for him. I went and bathed on the nearby pool just to take off the smell so I could face the day with courage. I went job hunting on restaurants, shops and supermarkets but to no avail, some would even insult me and chase me off like I was some kind of a rabies-infected dog. I needed nothing but a place to get a cent to be able to buy my unborn child some clothing. I was even willing to be a shop keeper, the kind of a job I had never dreamed of doing during my sweetest days with my family.

****

Those days were as bitter as overheated chili to my taste; I spent the whole week homeless. I was the talk of the town, the center of attraction, a smelly rose, a cruel angel. I had found a squatter camp where I lived alone without a thing. I had never imagined myself as a street kid, but I turned to be one, with the kids thinking I was mad or something, laughing at me, mocking me and throwing stones and bottles at me. My life was so painful and I was blocked on the hospital gate every time I tried to visit my mother. I had no clue whether she was still alive or not since I had no connection with anybody from home. Janet had cared for me but she would not leave our dying mother to care for the perpetrator it would never be fair. After a week in pain, I searched but would not find the reason to leave, all the prayers I recited to God every minute I felt they were worthless. My name was blotted out from the book of good souls, I belonged to hell. Those were my saddest thoughts as the shadows of death hung over me waiting to devour me; I saw it useful that I take my own life. I no longer had a heart, no soul there was only the body and the willing spirit, but I was done for.

There was a nearby river and I decided to throw myself there, I had never gathered courage to commit suicide before but I felt like what was the point of living when God rejected my every prayer? I walked slowly, saying goodbye to the world. I sat on a little rock just besides the river with a mind of committing suicide and killing both me and my child. The river flowed very harshly; it was loaded with all sorts of dirt and huge sticks. I was scared but I felt like I needed to do it, I wished I could see God stopping me from doing it, I wished He could save me because I believed I wanted to die but in reality I wanted to be saved. I got closer to the bank of the river and stood with my arms stretched, giving up on my life. What was the point of living when I had lost all I thought mattered to me, my home, my family, friends and my faith too? I shed my tears but I knew death was better for me, no heavy guilt, no shame and no pain. I would sleep peacefully in my grave not hearing the noise of people shattering down my world. I heard the sound of the feet moving at the nearby bushes and I ran toward the rock I had been sitting on. An old man with rugged clothes appeared looking tired and hungry. He came straight to me and I wiped my tears and smiled at him.

"How are you sir?" I greeted him first. I was a monster but I never forgot my manners.

"I'm well my child, you seem lonely," he sat beside me on a separate rock, his clothes were stinky.

"I am lonely sir, I'm homeless,"

"Oh. I'm sorry my child, what happened to you?" he was carrying an axe and he started sculpting some sticks. I related the whole story to him from scratch.

"So that's why my mom showed me out sir," I was crying and he had stopped sculpting. He took me in his rough arms and laid me on his lap. I did not spit on the smell but endured. It felt good having someone to tell my problems to.

"I won't lie to you baby, what you did was really wrong but I believe you've learnt from your mistakes now," he brushed my cheek with his hand. He was feeling for me.

"I believe so too granny, but now that I've apologized to God. Why does it still hurt? Why is He still punishing me? Two weeks have passed now and I'm still staying on the streets. He said it in the bible that no one is perfect but why is He being so severe on me like this?" I questioned him like he was God.

"My child, the Bible says God punishes the people He loves and in some situations we just blame God instead of ourselves and the devil himself. The devil served a temptation to you on a silver platter and you could not resist it during your holy night. Where there's God the devil comes and tries to disturb, my daughter. You've described your cousin as muscular and handsome and the devil might somehow have made you fall in love with those features that you don't see a man without those manly enough for you, but the devil leaves after leaving you in hell. He's not here to comfort you now but he was your best friend when you thought you were crazily in love with your cousin," my mind opened and I realized every bit of a thing that the man was saying.

"But granny, I prayed to God about this temptation after he broke my virginity. Why didn't He answer me before that? Why did He allow me to sink to it after that?" I asked.

"Where God is, the devil interferes; he would do anything in his power to make sure he wins you over. You prayed but you didn't have faith that God will rescue you. With God comes faith and with the devil comes fear. You used the wrong tactic of ignoring your feelings, pretending to hate him. You should have faced the tune with faith and courage because the devil doesn't have power over   God. He serves temptations but when He sees God interfering he runs. You should have been truthful and straight, but you used lies and hate to cover up your lust. You shouldn't have tried to protect a sin by sinning more," I exhaled, the page of my life was being revealed to me in front of me.

"Granny, I understand every word you say and I now understand fully how these two works. I have failed God. I wish He will forgive me someday," I shed a tear.

"God has already forgiven you my dear, He loves you more than you know and He rejoices that you regret your mistakes. He doesn't rejoice in your suffering and will give you a second chance in your life. Just trust in Him and have faith," he smiled at me as I moved from his lap and sat straight.

"Granny, do you think I really do have a second chance to a happy life, do you think I can still be able to live the life of my dreams?" I folded my legs on the rock and stared at him, hungry for more truth and more wisdom.

"Hundred percent grandchild! You're too young to think you're done for. You still have a great life ahead of you. Be true to yourself, replace your fears with your faith and pray for more courage and strength to take steps one day at a time. You might be scared of the world but they will do nothing but talk, you still have a chance to build your image, to restore your reputation and to chase your dreams freely. You're still breathing which means God still delights in you. Don't be afraid because He's always with you."

"Granny I can't thank you enough, I've been hungry to hear such words, now here you're saving my soul from hell," I was getting so comfortable with that man. "Anything for you dearest. And remember God cannot be fooled; God cannot be used as a shield to cover sins but can be used as a shield against sins and the devil. Never say you're Godly and never judge anyone who is not. People will judge you the way you judge them and you know that sins befalls anybody, we're all fallible. Be true to yourself and people around you and remember you cannot do some things without God. Pray for wisdom and courage, pray for confidence and for inner peace. With God you can go miles but the devil will entertain you and leave you halfway. Your cousin is not with you now, he should've cared enough to protect you and the baby in your womb, it was not love baby it was all lust. Love is never driven by emotions and wild feelings," he exhaled and took my hand in his; I was smiling and crying all at once, the tears were of joy.

"But I don't think I'll ever love again granny after all through this, no man will ever put their trust in me."

"As I've already told you about faith and second chances, it's all possible with God. You can't speak of love now dear, you've never loved or been loved. That was lust at its worst. Love doesn't work that way, it's real, and it's true and its patient. God grants love and the devil grants lust, lust ends bitterly, leaves heartbreaks and voids within the soul, but love is there all the time. Love bears, endures and lasts till death. It's not all about sex and six-packs, it comes from the heart. It cares about the happiness of each other."

I wondered where such an amazing man had rained from to wake me up from my darkest grave, I had believed I had known God but that day I believed I knew nothing about him. I was in the darkness, thick darkness.

"So granny, you mean I'll live happily ever after? You mean everything will just get flashed on the drainage just like that?" he laughed, I was fantasizing a lot.

"Baby, where there was once a wound a scar will always show up. The scar is never a sign of the weakness of the flesh but a sign of its strength. The scar means you survived, you're no longer hurting and you've defeated the pain and whatever what trying to break you. The scar will be there to remind you of the pain you once felt, it will remind you to never ever go back to that same field. The scar is just there to show you defeated the devil; the scar is your unborn child. Love him with all your heart and never look at him as a fruit of your mistakes but rather a blessing that rained down from heaven to awoken your sleeping magnificence."

"My God is an awesome God!" I smiled tearfully.

"He indeed is a marvelous God! A mysterious one don't you think?" We both laughed and it felt so good to be fueled with so much wisdom that kept my stuck soul to be willing to move again with life. Staying in the bushes feeling pity for myself was not going to work for me. I was not a failure. I was just an imperfect human being in an imperfect world.

"But that man kept promising to marry me, I thought he meant it, it sounded real," I said as I thought of Sydney.

"All he ever did was sleep with you, he wanted sex, men will do anything and say any lies for sex,"

"How do you know all these things granny?" I laughed.

"The Bible grandchild, that's my only tool. I live by it and I read lots of motivational books because I know this world is too cold and has lots of theories that will murder your head. The bible is the only thing that will make you live peacefully, make it your shield. It has every solution to your every problem. Live by it always."

"Thank you very much granny. Thank you for motivating me, for showing me the right path. I believe I will be able to walk on without any fear now. Thank you granny," I kissed his cheek. I no longer felt him stinky because I felt like hugging him so tightly. He was shivering a bit.

"Are you alright?"

"I'm feeling so thirsty dear, I believe it's because I came so far by feet. Get me some water," I ran towards the river to get him water with that sculpture he made that resembled a plate. He drank water and asked me to lay him down as he was losing his power. I was starting to feel scared but I gathered some courage because I was all alone there. I matted some tree branches on the rocky ground and took his axe and peeled some tree banks which I was taught could heal fever. I mixed that with water and made him drink. He stopped shaking and smiled.

"You'll be a doctor someday," I was relieved he was well again. I slept besides him and he told me lots of stories and motivational words.

"I want to be a public speaker from now," we both giggled.

"So granny, where do you come from? I didn't even ask you that, I was busy with my painful stories."

"As you can see how shabby I am my child, I neither have a wife nor kids. I come from a nearby rural village. I live alone in a small hut and I survive with sculpting," I shed a tear, feeling for him, my pains were nothing compared to his.

"I'm very sorry granny. I will move in with you to my mansion someday," he laughed.

"You don't need to worry about me grandchild, I have everything I need. Everything believe me," he laid his head on a rock.

"I believe you granny, as long as you have God, you have everything you need, " I smiled at the thought that he has passed his every piece of wisdom to me.

"That's my girl. Let's sleep now you talk too much," I laughed my lungs out and he laughed too. I tied my hand around his aged body full of wrinkles and he put his hand on my head in adoration.   That had been the happiest, most amazing, most important and the most useful moment of my life. I heard him snoring loudly and I smiled and dozed off to sleep. I had nothing but had everything.

CHAPTER FOURTEEN

I was with someone else when I opened my eyes, I remembered
I had been at the river bank the previous night, I had expected to

wake up with my newly found grandpa by my side, him feeding me wisdom but he was not there. I was with a young man instead, in his apartment; it was a large place with the most stunning furnishings ever. I was sleeping on a king sized bed with the smooth blankets. The time by which I woke up shown me I had slept like a baby, because it had been long since I last had slept on bed. I had been used to rocks and river banks, or the grass. It was eleven o'clock and as a hard working girl I had never woke up at eleven, six o'clock had always been my time. I missed being at home, I missed mom even though I knew I had murdered every chance of waking up next to her. My infidelity had taken all precious and valuable things away from me. I had to face it, it was my entire fault but where was my new grandfather?

"Good morning cutie, you slept like a baby," Travis's voice, for the first time, sounded like music to my ears causing the radiation of a smile through my cute face, the exact thing I needed the most.

"How did I get here?" I sat up on bed and faced him; my eyes roaming around the whole house in admiration.

"I searched for you. I've been searching for you since that day I told you to come sleep at my place," he put his arms around me and planted a kiss on my cheek I smiled.

"How did you find me then, where is the man I was with?" I was amazed by the sudden confidence in my voice.

"You're too inquisitive Jay! Just relax okay," he patted my shoulders.

"Not until you tell me where you threw my husband to," his eyes widened.

"So that's your husband," I laughed a lot.

214

"Of course sir where's he?"

"Judging by the posture you guys slept, I can agree to that one," we both laughed.

"Well maybe you need to bath before I show you to him."

"That's true, I stink."

He smiled and got off the bed and showed me the bathroom. It was a huge bathroom with tall mirrors and two bathtubs. I was used to a shower but I had always loved bathtubs, we did not have one at home. Starring at the mirror, I was amazed about how dirty I was and the snow white walls, sinks and tubs made it worse. I looked at my stomach; it had popped out a little in my dress. My hair was a real mess, with sand and small pieces of grass and mud. I wondered how Travis still managed to hug me, kiss me or put me to sleep in such a condition. I scrubbed myself with so much severity not caring whether the skin would peel off like a banana. I noticed the water turning brown with dirt hence I showered twice or thrice. I combed my hair and tied it neatly after bathing, I felt so smooth and I washed my clothes. I looked at myself on the mirror and I still looked beautiful. I applied lotions and perfumed my body. I also brushed my teeth a thousand times. I felt fresh and smooth after that. I regretted ever trying to kill myself and smiled at myself. I still had a chance in life. God had shown me that. I wore Travis' shirt that was hanged on the hanger and went out of the bathroom. He was in the dining room busy setting up dishes on the dining table. He stopped and looked at me as I approached; smiled and slowly progressed towards me with open arms.

"I've never seen such beauty before," I closed my eyes blushing and went and fell on his arms.

"You're simply exaggerating to make me feel good, I look like the prodigal son when he got back from wasting his riches," he laughed his lungs out.

"At least that's my favorite part, the prodigal son still came back!" he said.

The hug was different from Sydney's, it had no wild intentions, and it was warm and full of love.

"I failed to live without you Jay. I thought about you every second and I regret ever letting you go or thinking ill of you," his voice was real but full of pain.

"I'm the one who's supposed to be regretting right now, for confusing infatuation with love. For ever trying to misuse a piece that my puzzle is incomplete without," we stared at each other for long, and for the first time I felt love from deep within. I was smiling endlessly like an idiot and he laughed at me.

"What happened Jay? You still don't look like someone who would do that," he pulled a chair and sat down, I did too.

"I made a mistake by thinking I could be perfect on my own. I thought I was perfect, I wanted so bad to believe it, but I was wrong, no one is perfect. It's so sad I had to learn the hard way and it'll probably take some time before I completely heal and forgive myself."

"I forgive you Jay. I don't know why but I love you, of course that perfect Jay I always seen has been erased from my mind and I see you for who you are and I know you won't repeat the same mistake again," he assured me and I thanked him for opening doors for me once again when the world was giving up on me.

"Now as much as I would like to sit here and enjoy watching your cute teeth chew this food, I have to bath so I can take you to your man," he left after kissing my forehead.

"Now you are talking," I was not sure whether he heard me or not because he was gone beyond earshot. There was a mouth-watering breakfast before me, three slices of toast bread, with sausages, scrambled eggs, polony and hot coffee. I thanked the heavens that Travis had gone to bath or else I would not have enjoyed my meal. I chopped onto the food so hungrily, it had been long since I had last ate anything delicious because I lived in the squatters and sometimes on the rocks near the river. I shuffled everything in till I was hundred percent sure my stomach needed no more food. I went to that breath taking kitchen, everything was well set. The walls were also white while the cupboards were wooden brown and shiny. The tiles were white and wooden too. The essence there could make you fade off to sleep. I swore Travis' parents knew how to choose their furniture. He approached while I was roaming around admiring their home. He was carrying a new plastic bag with some things inside. He was wearing an ebony dark suit with white shirt and a red tie and black polished pointed shoes. His hair neatly laid to the front side, beards neatly shaved and connected to his sideburns. His brown colored face flashing and pink lips curved in a hot smile. After the food he had served me with, he made my mouth watery too.

"Wow you look handsome," I stood still.

"Thank you Jay,"

"Forgive me but I can't stop admiring this place and I forgot to even ask about your parents. Where are they?" I blushed. "This is my new apartment, I moved out of theirs," he said.

"Why would you? You're not married yet. You're still young."

"I heard you were wandering around the streets and I informed them about it. I asked them to let you move in with us, they rejected the offer and I rented this apartment so I could let you in," I held my mouth amazed.

"Travis! You shouldn't have rejected your family because of me, I'm not worth it!" he moved closer and stood behind me and tied his hands around my waist.

"I can do anything for the person I love," he pecked my lips and gave me a warm hug.

"But Trav, you shouldn't have," I was saddened by the fact that I had made a guy brawl with his parents, all which could not have happened if I had behaved myself.

"I'm sorry dear; I'm the reason for all this."

"Don't worry honey; just promise me you'll never do anything of that sort ever again," he said as he raised my chin and gazed straight at my face.

"I'm scared of making promises now darling, I've realized there is nobody perfect except God and I know the pain of breaking people's trust in me. I love you and I will keep on trying to behave every day," a tear rolled down my left eye. "Wow, someone has matured now," he smiled as he wiped off the tear with his right thumb and I smiled back.

"I love you Trav."

"I know right," he laughed.

"Now take these clothes and go change. We need to go please hurry; I'll be outside washing my car," he handed me the plastic bag and went outside. I hurried to the bedroom wondering where we were going. I voiced my awe looking at the clothes he had bought for me. A black skinny and long sleeved maxi dress with red high heels, a silver watch and a matching silver clutch bag. I looked really beautiful after trying them on. My slim body and my not-so-huge curves showed up gracefully on their right places with my baby appearing so tiny in front. I did comb my hair for the second time and I looked incredible without trying too hard. The walls shook as I moved and I felt pride once again in myself, he was waiting for me in the gate. The cottage was surrounded with green glistening lawn and different colored flowers; there was a small pool just beside the aisle that led to the gate. That house was really beautiful and a handsome man stood with his eyes glued to that little beautiful creature that approached him.

"I won't say no more that you're beautiful. Should I say it?" he scooped me in his arms, pecked my lips and opened the door for me while throwing me with total care in his Porsche and I moaned a littles he closed the door and got in. Staring at me with affectionate eyes, he switched on the engine and started off and in his car radio and played Brian Adam's song 'Please forgive me'. Tears would not stop falling from my eyes as he took the way to the hospital. His left hand rested on my right lap and my hands were scratching it softly while my mind got deeply lost in the love song being played.

He switched off the engine and I had not realized we had reached the hospital. He took my hands and kissed them. I watched him with love and affection.

"Baby, let's get in," I watched the hospital yard with so much, what had happened to my granny or was it mom? In total silence I got off the car and he led the way to the male ward. I grabbed him from behind.

"Trav is everything alright?"

"Just follow me baby," I trailed behind him and he took me to the ward that had my grandfather. He was seated in bed and I rushed and held him tight. He smiled tearfully to me and tears rolled down my eyes.

"Granny what's wrong? Why are you here?" I sat beside him and wrapped my arm around him.

"I'm sick baby and I believe my time has come and I wanted so bad to talk to you before I die." Fear struck through me once again, he had just become a part of my life but he was talking about dying.

"No granny, you're not going to die until I buy a mansion. I promised to take you with me remember," I smiled tearfully. "My daughter, I can't change the hands of time. I love you a lot," there were shadows that approached the ward as he was speaking and I did not mind them as I focused on my dying grandfather. Travis was standing with his hands in his pocket leaning on the wall besides the bed where we sat and was watching us and feeling the pain with us.

"Please take good care of yourself. Don't forget anything that I told you last night. Apply my words to your life everyday and you will prosper in everything you do. Never forget God, God is the pillar of your strength; God is all you need and never ever repeat confusing love with the infatuation. Know the difference with these two and you will live long. I have a very precious gift for you, it's in the locker. Take it with you until you die, never lose it. You have become my daughter since I've told you I have no children, God has not granted them to me. I have delighted in you, I still believe in you even if the world is against you. May you find true peace once again in your life, may you find true love and may your mother and the rest of the family forgive you. I love you dear. Lay me down to sleep now and take this with you home," he drew the locker and handed me the Holy Bible. I was trembling with fear and and the area of my dress in my chest was wet with tears and sweat. Travis came and sat next to me and brushed my shoulders in comfort.

"Call the doctor Trav! How could you sit here?" I screamed but Travis did not move. Granny held my hands and rubbed them softly.

"Don't worry baby and please don't cry you're hurting me if you do. I told you to be strong... death has no power over... God..." I put his head on my two little hands and watched him battle for his spirit as it slowly departed from him. I kept my peace as his head rested on my lap and the storm calmed. "Doctor please, Get over here!" I shouted in tears, rolled my mouth in sorrow and wept bitterly. Travis left and called the nurses to take care of the corpse, I was still weeping like a crazy person for my new best friend who had left just like that. My head was facing down and I had my hands on my head while weeping so painfully, Travis was shedding tears but was trying so hard to be strong for me. As I raised my eyes, there was mom and Janet standing behind me. I wiped off my tears surprised on how they got there, with my mouth wide open, Janet came and sat next to me and hugged me. I had missed her a lot.

"Jenny!"

"Sis Jay," we hugged so tightly and mom watched us. She was still in a hospital gown and I was sure she was still admitted but she looked completely fine to me. I was embarrassed to face her at some point but I gathered courage and went to hug her. I thought she was going to ignore me but she progressed towards me and scooped me in her arms weeping.

"Jasmine! my baby!"

"I'm sorry mom, please forgive me," I lamented.

"I'm sorry too baby!" I knew mom had heard the words of my old granny and they had touched her at some point, they made her regret disowning me.

"No mom, you were angry and you did what every woman would've done after being betrayed that much. I still love you mom, a lot."

It was both awkward and awesome reuniting with my family but I was glad to be a new soul. I realized how much I had missed my mom's arms. My mistakes were going to steal that from me if I had allowed them. Janet was smiling continuously and Travis too biting his lower lip. Jenny kept on winking her eye at me questioning about me and Travis being back together. I was smiling and nodding my head in agreement that I indeed was in love with him. Mom was overwhelmed with joy because Travis was her dream son-in-law. I wished my first born could have been Travis' but there was no turning back. The nurses took the body to the mortuary. I was glad at some point that granny was at peace, and he has left me in a better place. I sat down with mom, Travis and Jenny and related the story on how I met the man and how much he had taught me. Mom was glad seeing that I was regretting my actions.

"Baby, you should phone the man's relatives and inform them about his death," Travis whispered to me as we left the ward and with our hands intertwined.

"He doesn't have anyone dear. I will take care of everything even if I don't know how but I will try," I wanted his help so bad; I had nothing to assist with, only my heart and my soul and probably a few words to say at his funeral.

"Oh I'm sorry love, I didn't know. I will help you out with everything you need okay?" he brushed my back.

"Thank you dear."

"And you may come back home honey, you're totally welcome," mom said as she flashed a brighter smile. Mom was going to be discharged that evening from the hospital and she was waiting for her medications. Many eyes were glued to me as we walked on the hospital corridors, patients and nurses who knew me had expected to see me in rugged and shabby clothes but they were surprised to see me smart and still cute. I thanked Travis in my heart. His love was so true after everything I had done to him he still saw a girlfriend in me. We spent the day at Travis place with Janet who could not stop admiring the place the way I had done before.

"Sis Jay, we should spend the night over here. What do you think?" she was sleeping on a furry huge couch and eating raisin biscuits and sipping on yoghurt with a straw and I was reading the bible on a separate couch.

"No more sleepovers for me, they destroyed my life," I laughed.

"And besides, we won't sleep today we'll have to make preparations for my granny's funeral tomorrow."

"You've just reminded me, we need to go and buy a coffin now and takeaways now," Travis said as he approached the lounge.

"Oh yeah that."

"Please leave me here; I need to rest a bit" said Janet as she closed her eyes and pretended to snow. We laughed and passed her by and went on with shopping all the necessities for the funeral.

****

"Unfortunately, we all here aren't familiar with the man we're burying today. I believe I'm the only one who knows his story that's the reason why I carried out everything for his burial..." I was given a chance to speak at granny's funeral and all the eyes were cursing me as I stood up. Our church members were mumbling and casting evil eyes on me but I kept my confidence as I remembered what the man had told me about the world and judging other people. Some even wanted to leave and some shouted at the Master of ceremony for even offering me a loud speaker to say my peace.

"We're here for some important work not to let this little brat spoil the day. What do we do with people who sleep with their cousins here?" one man shouted from the crowd and interrupted me as I tried speaking. Mom, Travis and Janet we're there for me. Mercy and Cheryl were also there with their parents and our church members were also gathered there. Nobody wanted anything to do with me except mom, Jenny and Travis.

"I know that I'm the last person you want to hear from right now. I know you think I stink because of my sins and my mistakes. I don't really blame you because it's all my fault but I won't spend the rest of my life hiding in a corner because I committed this horrible mistake. This man on this coffin here, the man who taught me how life goes and even granted me this confidence of standing in front of you today speaking, may his precious soul rest in peace," there was a deafening silence.

"Judge me all you want and call me all sorts of names but I've already apologized to my God and I know I've been granted a second chance in the affairs of life. I'm not proud of my behaviors and I know I messed up. I broke the trust of all those who believed in me, especially my mother and my little sister. They had been nothing but blessings to me, but today I know all of you question my mother's parenting. Mom is one of the best parents in this world and she did everything she had to do just to make sure I was well-mannered, but the fault is with me, I was never true to her. I was never true to myself too and to all those around me. I faked myself and succumbed everyday to temptations," I saw my mother crying and Janet too.

"I no longer have friends even though I had been blessed with the best of them, I betrayed them and it came as a surprise to them because they never knew I was capable of doing that. I entertained my sins and they bombarded me in the end. I cherished sin and made it my friend and most of all, I used God's name to cover up my sins. I confused lust and love; I could've never fallen in love with my cousin. I thought I loved him, I thought I knew it all but I was mistaken. The man in this coffin made me realize that," I was so emotional that the whole crowd, especially women started crying.

"Instead of judging me, may you please teach your children to know the difference between good and evil. Teach them the difference between when it's God and when it's Satan. It might be them tomorrow. Nobody had known I was capable of doing such a disgusting thing, but I did it anyway. We live in a cold world where Satan lures God's people and drags them into pain every day. I thought I prayed, I thought I knew God, I judged my friends and called them devilish, I thought I was Godly but now I understand I had never known God. If I had prayed truly I wouldn't be here today, if I had been Godly I wouldn't be confessing anything right here. But here I am, my granny taught me one thing, that there's nothing impossible with God, that I have a second chance in life and that if I entertain the devil he will keep dancing around me. I love my God and I've been blessed. My mother has forgiven me, God has already granted me true love and I know some of you are judging Travis for taking me back while I'm pregnant with my cousin's child. Travis loves me and I know it, I knew it even the day I betrayed him but as I said that I failed to differentiate between evil and good. I no longer have anything more to say. The rest, you'll find it in the Bible, may my Granny's soul rest in perfect peace. Thank you."

There was clapping of hands and mom came to hug me tightly as I sat down next to her. Cheryl and Mercy came and hugged me too and even Mercy's mom came to me and apologized to me. I understood the meaning of, 'you shall know the truth and the truth shall set you free.' Many people came and shook hands with me and I felt great for making that speech. However some of them still saw me as a wolf in sheep's clothing. I did not care much; I was still trying to gain my confidence and to forgive myself for my mistakes. I knew mom's trust and her love for me were never going to be the same but I was glad however that the fire was cooled. She was even happier that Travis had accepted me even if I was still stained with the most horrible stains but he still took me back to him.

"You whore!" a hoarse unfriendly voice came from the crowd and I saw a woman approaching me. It was Travis' mother, the headmistress and our church member; she was a huge chubby woman. I knew she was never friendly with so many people.

"If you think you can fool my child and drag him into your messy life, you'll have me to deal with! You may fool all of them here but definitely not me!" she grabbed me by the hand and in a short time people were gathered around us. She had created a worst scenario.

"Leave her alone mom!" Travis pushed her away and she nearly fell onto the ground. Mom and Janet held me tight and moved me away from the crowd. I was angered by that woman's actions.

"Travis! you're pushing your own mother just because of this whore? You're even protecting another man's baby. You amaze me, you're blinded by lust for this stupid useless brat, I can't wait to see you regret once again when she leaves you for his cousin," she shouted from behind and left for her car red with anger. Travis bit his lips and followed us to his car.

"Thank you for rescuing me babe," I said calmly.

"Don't mind her, she's always like this, she'll be fine soon," he consoled me and we drove off. The funeral was done with and I was glad to have done such a great job. We spent the day at Travis apartment and went back home by evening.

CHAPTER FIFTEEN

"You haven't told me when Aunt left Jenny?" I said as I prepared eggs for breakfast with my little sister washing the dishes and cleaning the cupboards at our home. Mom was still obn bed.

"I really forgot sis Jay, she went back to her home right after mom had woke up from her coma," something was upsetting her I could read her face.

"Why would she leave so early? She was supposed to stay till her recovery," I said stirring my egg soup on the frying pan.

"Actually dear, mom and aunt are no longer on talking terms. Aunt started blaming you for everything and mom came to your rescue. Mom blamed the both of you but aunt kept on saving Sydney saying he is innocent in all this. That's when the argument was heated and they fought to an extent of aunt leaving and promising to never set foot here ever again," she confessed sadly and I took a long breath in realization of how much harm I had caused in my family.

"I feel bad for this entire thing Jenny; it will really take time to forgive myself. I'm the reason behind everything."

"I'm sorry sis, I'm just glad you're home with me and that there is peace between us as a family," she came and hugged me.

"And thank you for supporting mom Jenny; she couldn't have done it alone," we smiled, the time for weeping and mourning was over. We had to build our lives, our courage and our strength.

"Yeah, I've been the good girl, the bad part of me died because I learnt a lot from your mistakes sis, I learnt a lot from them and I never want to cause mom any stress again. No alcohol for me, no marijuana, no parties and no clubbing. I've got to be a good aunt to my little Jaden," I was so overwhelmed with enthusiasm hearing of my sister's great transformation and I laughed. "I just can't wait for the new you young sis," we laughed together precariously.

"As for me, I'm already in love with the new you."

"But who's Jaden now Jenny?" I asked with a puzzled look. "He's my little unborn boy," she came and brushed my tummy softly and lovely.

"This one will get whatever he needs; he's my number one child," I was blushing at my little sister's love for my unborn baby.

"Oh seems like I no longer have to worry about anything since this child has two mothers already."

"He has only one mother!" mom smiled as she approached the kitchen from her bedroom.

"And that's me," we all laughed.

"Mom, you won't be able to raise this one, I already see how naughty he'll be, breaking things and running around everywhere," Jenny said as she placed the dishes on a tray to serve breakfast to mom.

"That's exactly what I love about kids. I'll tell Travis that this baby is mine. Jay you'll leave this one with me, he's mine," I knew mom was serious about the matter. She never wanted me to be troubled by baby matters in my marriage. She wanted me to start a new life with Travis. I wished I had given my virginity to him.

"I don't have a problem with that mom," I smiled as we all sat down around the table and helped ourselves on bread, eggs and hot coffee.

"I'm the happiest woman alive to have the two of you, thank you for not allowing circumstances to break us up. I love you a lot for this my kids. I'm glad you're here and you're happy again," mom said with tearful eyes. I could read joy and peace in her mind.

"And mom, we thank you for being so humble, so kind and so strong for us. If it were somebody else, they wouldn't be able to handle the pressure. I also want to apologize for causing enmity between you and aunt."

"It's okay baby, she'll come around at some point. I'm just happy we're all alive and safe," we hugged as a group, laughed and had a lovely moment as a family.

"And baby, about the university deal. I did not cancel it; you are still going next month. You'll come back for delivery when the time comes," I did not know where I got the wings but I had flown to my mother in just a second and hugged her so tight I could feel her bones cracking.

"Mom thank you very much!" I had tears on my eyes and I could not help it. I was sad I had to go to school with my pregnancy but I was glad that I still had a chance to complete my education and chase my dreams.

"So has Sydney contacted you yet?" mom asked with a mouthful of bread.

"I don't want to hear from him mom, I just don't want to talk to him," I could feel anger and embarrassment rising within me at the mention of his name.

"You should let go of that anger within you baby, if he calls you, pick the phone and hear him out. Anger won't help anymore. He might need his baby."

"I will do so mom," I quickly obeyed mom's word just to roll past the topic. I went to rest in our bedroom after breakfast and left Jenny with the dishes and mom went for a walk to exercise her body. Looking around the room I wished I could rewind the time and undo everything I had done with Sydney. I took a long breath and threw myself at the bed. I was about to doze off to sleep when Jenny rushed into the room with mom's phone ringing.

"Jay, Sydney is calling."

"Answer Jenny, I don't want to speak to him," I turned around and faced an opposite direction from Jenny who answered the call and said a few words before handing the phone to me. I never wanted to take it but I obeyed mom's words when she said I was supposed to talk to him.

"Hello," I said reluctantly.

"You still have a beautiful voice baby, I missed you," I nearly crashed the phone but I held my breath.

"What do you want from me?"

"Well, I just want to apologize for leaving you in that hell alone. I heard you had no place to live and you were roaming around the streets. I'm sorry."

"Well thank you sir. I'm fine now. I'm hanging up."

"Wait, don't be stubborn I'm still talking to you. I heard you're back with Travis but you know I won't allow that guy to raise my baby. I want him so you'll have to hand him over to me after deliverance," I felt hot air coming out of my nostrils.

"You're crazy, this is my baby and he will live with my mother! Period."

"Well Jay, this is just not up for discussion. My baby will live with me. Period," he hung up the phone and left me hanging. I had millions of reasons for hating Sydney. He was just arrogant. I realized how much of the devil he was. I threw the phone on the bed and dozed off to sleep. I was awoken by mom who had arrived.

"What did he say baby?" she sat on the bed besides me.

"Says he wants his baby mom. I hate him."

"Hating him is not the solution, forgive him and move on with your life. You have a baby that connect you guys and this hatred just won't work," I understood what mom was saying.

"But mom, since you and aunt are not on talking terms do you think she will treat my child with love?"

"Sydney doesn't stay with his mom, he has his apartment, I doubt they even connect well now," that statement chilled my insides and I knew there was no battle I would win against Sydney. Handing the baby would be an advantage to my studies and my relationship with Travis too.

"That's way better mom."

"And you need to start packing; you have to leave tomorrow for school."

"Who needs fairy godmothers when she has a mother like mine?" I praised her as I slid from the bed to pack all the necessary things for my studies.

"You're still sweet! I thought you'd be vulnerable," we laughed our lungs out and Janet came to join us.

"We need to pray so that the devil doesn't come and attempt to steal this joy we have right now," mom said as we all knelt and communicated with our heavenly Father.

CHAPTER SIXTEEN

I heard the screeching of brakes and a car hooting noisily at the gate. The gate alarm was also ringing continually, it was annoying. I fidgeted and tossed on the bed reluctant to wake up but the alarm went beyond merely ringing to screaming. Defeated, I threw the blankets over my husband, rubbed my eyes and shook him.

"Honey, do you hear that noise?" I hated myself for waking him up; he had had a long meeting with his fellow doctors the previous day. He also had to pick up Janet and mom from the airport as I was also giving therapy to my suicidal and mentally unstable patients of mine.   "What? What's the wrong bunny?" he stretched himself slowly and turned to look at me.

"There is a car hooting outside and I'm sure it's at our gate," I said as I left the bed to wrap a body towel around my body.

"Wait, where's the security guard at?" Trav peeped through the window.

"Bunny, what time could it be? Jaden and his little sister are already outside playing in the gardens," I went and stood beside him and peeped outside, our two kids were playing nicely on our flowery and rainbow-colored garden. Jaden was six years old and had learned to water every flower in the garden and he was driving his toy car carrying his little sister Jermyn. I wished with a bleeding heart that Jaden had been Travis' son. The sun was already up in the sky and the flowers were glistening with water and the scene outside was breathtaking.

"They love each other so much honey don't they?" I smiled at my husband who rubbed my back and stamped a kiss on my forehead relaxing my soul.

"Let's just say we know we have beautiful kids and we're a beautiful family," we laughed.

We were the happiest family ever. We lived with our two kids, Jaden (Sydney's and mine son) and Jermyn our second-born daughter (mine and Travis' kid), our maid and cook, Mrs. Rodney; we had Trevor our security guard, in California, Los Angeles in North America. I had started varsity pregnant, gave birth at school, and gave my son Jaden to my mother who stayed with him and supported him until I finished my varsity and obtained my degree in Clinical Psychology. Travis had completed his master's degree at the University of Zimbabwe and applied for a job as a Medical doctor in North America where he got it. I got married to Travis just after finishing my studies, we had a white wedding and mom was the happiest woman alive. We moved to America after my husband had gotten a job since I failed to live with his mother who hated me with all she had but used to love me before my shenanigans, every action has its consequences. We lived in a huge mansion, nine-roomed, with a garden, an orchard and two swimming pools. I was paying for Janet's school fees at the University of Zimbabwe as she was studying Law there. She and mom visited us frequently during her holidays since mom had retired and my husband had bought her a house in Harare. Our lives were a little fairytale at the moment and I believed that it was true that if you believe that God has forgiven you for your sins, He grants you a second chance in life. I had the most wonderful and happiest family in the world and lived in my dream city.

My husband urged our gateman to check who the person at the gate was and open for them. We stood at the window with our eyes glued at the gate to see who the person and we watched a white, shiny Lamborghini sliding into our home.

"Who could it be? Didn't you settle your debt with the Bank Manager?" I asked my husband with a puzzled look.

"I have no idea babe, we fixed everything yesterday maybe he has something else to say or maybe it's the Jaden's Principal, that man is just troublesome. He demands endlessly. Get dressed bunny."

"I know him. New uniforms and whatnots," I said laughing. Trav grabbed his faded jeans and white t-shirt and went out. I went to the dressing room and pulled out jeans, a white vest and put on my morning slippers. I trailed behind my husband as we walked downstairs to our aristocratic lounge. Our maid and cook Mrs. Rodney had already mopped the floor and everything was in place. A taller guy we could see standing just outside our glassy burglars.

"That's not the bank manager," Travis whispered.

"Then who could it be?" I moved closer and opened the door. I felt like my eyes were betraying me. I could not believe that the tall man at my door was Sydney, Jaden's father and my cousin. I was still surprised since five years had passed and now my son was schooling and he had disappeared to God-knows-where.

"Will you let me in or will you just stand and gawk at me like this forever?" his voice was a bit hoarse but it had not changed a lot, just an addition of bass and he has beards in his face.

"Oh come in," I moved out of the way as he marched in with his hands in his pocket, I swore with all I had, Jaden was mine and I was never going to hand my son over to a careless father. My husband loved him and treated him as his own, just the same as my second born female child Jermyn Tracy. Travis followed him and made him sit on the couch. I closed the door and went to join them.

"You may sit there; I'll prepare something for food," I said after warm greetings and stood up heading towards the kitchen.

"Wait! I'm not here for food; I'm just here for my son," he stood up and my husband did the same.

"Well as far as I know, there are procedures to be followed if you want him, you just don't barge in other people's home and boast like this," Trav warned.

"I don't follow any procedure. I'm here for my son. And don't you dare threaten me, I'm not scared of you remember!" You could swear Sydney's anger lived on his throat, it rose up so easily.

"I won't fight with you and I'm not threatening you, but this is my house and you won't disrespect me under my own roof and in front of my family!" Travis was boiling too. I felt bad; it was my fault that Travis and Sydney would not get along well. "The family you're talking about is my girlfriend and my son," his arrogance and pride would not stop. I felt like strangling him but then I remembered that I was the reason behind that hatred. I knew that my mistakes were not going to disappear in the air like that, but there were a lot of things that were going to remind me of my sins. I was just glad to have them as lessons; I never wanted to be threatened by them. "This scene you want to create over here is just unnecessary. I'm going to make breakfast then we'll settle matters peacefully," I interfered and then turned my back on them towards the kitchen and judging by the deafening silence behind me, they obeyed me. Travis was silenced by Sydney's words and I knew they hurt him. The fact that I once got in bed with my cousin was the worst nightmare to him. He kept quiet like that and never opened his mouth again. I hurt so bad seeing my husband being humiliated in front of me and because of me. I found our breakfast already prepared by our female cook Mrs. Rodney and ready to be served. I helped her carry the dishes to the dining table.

"Mommy, Jermyn won't stop crying. She fell from my toy car," my first born son Jaden approached the dining room holding his young sister's hand as I was just about to join Sydney and Travis on the dining table. Sydney stood up and hurried to lift him, he could see that he was his son because of the resemblance.

"My boy!" he planted kisses on his forehead and I rolled my eyes. The guy would not stop disrespecting us at our own premises. Jaden shook trying hard to free himself from Sydney, he was scared of him, he was not friendly with strangers, and that alone was inherited from Sydney.

"Daddy, come free me," he shouted at Travis who was sitting quietly at the table. Mom and Janet came in with groceries, they had visited us as. They both stood in awe seeing the drama that played at my house. I went and took Jaden from Sydney who was saddened by the fact that his own son was scared of him. We all sat down around the table quietly; after Janet had said a prayer we started helping ourselves to food. Everybody was quiet, only the clinching of spoons, forks and knives could be heard. My heart broke at I thought of losing my son to Sydney. I had thought Sydney had forgotten all about him and was glad to have built a family with Travis who loved Jaden as his. A tear slipped down my cheeks, it was my entire fault that my son was being taken away from me.

"Jaden, sitting beside you is your father, Sydney," I broke the silence and everybody starred at me and I focused on my son who flashed his confusion at me.

"No, my father is the one beside you mom," my son was rude, he said as he chopped his food with a fork and knife. I knew it was going to be hard convincing him that Sydney was his real father so I kept my cool. I stopped eating, I had lost my appetite.

"Well, aunt and everybody. I'm here for Jaden. I feel bad for having my son grow under someone else's roof while I'm alive but I had no choice since you all know I'm a businessman and I had to travel. I booked a flight to this place just to take my son with me," Sydney said with a determination that made me regret ever getting into bed with him. I closed my eyes and swallowed his words, knowing that was the end of my and my son's relationship.

"I thought you were going to at least apologize to me for impregnating my daughter, you just come and seize like you're Hitler," mom's forehead furrowed in anger.

"Well aunt, it's not like I forced my cousin into it. It was our fault, both of us, and she consented to it. Now Jay, if you may help me pack Jaden's clothes, our flight is at exactly one o'clock. We've got no time to waste," he said as he stood up. I searched for my husband's eyes which gave me that exact instruction because I could see he was fed up with sitting. The same table as Sydney. I stood up with total uneasiness and went to my son's room to pack his belongings. Sydney walked in on me, I was sobbing.

"Don't put too many clothes over there, he already has much waiting for him. Just pack two or three for the journey," he hated the fact that Travis had bought things for Jaden.

"Will you let me see him?" I asked in sobs and he came and sat in front of me.

"We'll do co-parenting just because I love you but I don't want my son near your husband that's the problem."

"Why do you hate Travis? He hasn't done anything to you. He loves Jaden as his own."

"He took you away from me, we were supposed to get married remember?" I knew he was trying to tempt me but I was shielded and would never allow myself to succumb to temptations again so I ignored him and handed him Jaden's bag reluctantly.

"Take care of my son, make sure he is well-fed and does not indulge in some thug life. Make sure he goes to church every day...." I gave him millions of instructions with pain striking me inwardly.

"Will you kiss me now and stop lecturing me about what or what to not do to my son, look what we brought into this world Jay," he moved closer to me and I pushed him back.

"Promise me you'll allow me to see my son my cousin," I begged.

"Why are you panicking baby? I would never do that to you, this son is ours and the fact that you bore him for me is priceless. Now give me a kiss c'mon," I moved away and out of the room as he trailed behind me. Janet had bathed Jaden and clothed him, Travis was seated with our daughter Jermyn on his lap and mom was picking the dishes from the dining table to the dishwasher. Our cook, Mrs. Rodney was sweeping the floor just below the table. Everyone wore sadness in their faces. Travis had had made a sweet, strong bond with Jaden, he was our treasure and my daughter was going to be lonely without his brother. I saw the consequences of my mistakes flashing in front of me like lightning. I took Jaden from Jenny and hugged him tightly.

"Baby, you're going with your father now. Mommy still loves you a lot, I will come and take you back and I will call you every day. Behave yourself honey. I love you so much. You'll be back soon!" I was mourning as I said goodbye to my son, Jenny and mom joined me along. Travis was still seated.

"Mommy, I don't want to go," cried Jaden as he pressed himself tightly to my arms.

"I know baby but you'll be fine. Daddy's taking you mountain climbing and swimming," I tried to smile even though my heart was breaking slowly.

"Really mom? Then I'll go!" he escaped my arms and ran to Sydney who smiled and lifted him and if human beings had photocopies, Sydney and Jaden would be the first one to be known of, they resembled each other from head to toe.

"Goodbye everyone. Wish you all a good life," Sydney waved as he slowly marched out of the room with happiness written all over his face. I sat on the couch and wept, I had wished to have my family under one roof with love and happiness but I had failed. Mom came and sat next to me, brushed my back.

"It's okay love. You haven't lost him forever, there are still ways to get him back especially through the court."

"The court will still arrange co-parenting for us mom, Sydney did not deny the pregnancy and he loves his child, he might use that to defend himself," I spoke slowly. Travis came and sat next to me and kissed my cheek and mom left us.

"It's okay bunny, we still have a chance to make more and more kids right?" he whispered and I smiled and lifted my eyes to look at him.

"Stupid! they won't be Jaden"

"I just wanted to see you smile and here you are," he laughed.

"I love you Trav, I wish I had loved only you from the start. I wish I had lost my virginity to you. I would be with Jaden right now," I rested my head on his chest and gazed at his eyes.

"Don't worry bunny, what's done is done. We can't reverse the time. I'm just glad I'm with you here, just glad you ended up where you were meant to be. And I'll help you get full custody of Jaden I promise you."

"Thank you, baby. I'm glad I've been enlightened about these entire life matters sweetie. The difference between love and lust, truth and lies, fake and real, betrayal and trust, failure and success, God and Satan, wisdom and folly I know it all. I wouldn't have known these if I had not made my mistakes. God gave me a second chance my love and I'm now able to separate good from evil, light from darkness...I know now that no one is perfect but God!"

"Dawn on your bunny!"

"Dawn on my honey!"

"Now follow me upstairs please!" my husband escaped my hands and ran upwards; I followed him sliding swiftly like a hungry snake, I was going to eat him alive.

THE END!

www.ingramcontent.com/pod-product-compliance
Lightning Source LLC
Chambersburg PA
CBHW051105030726
47504CB00006B/1797